She was supposed to be flirtatious.

To play the part of the moneygrubbing tart with loose morals he needed her to be, that his family would expect her to be. But right now she was shocked into immobility.

He moved his hands then, sliding them around the back of her neck, down between her shoulder blades, along the line of her spine until his hands spanned her waist. She arched, wishing she could press her body against his. Wishing she could do something to close the distance between them. Because he was still sitting in his chair and she in hers.

He pulled away, and she followed him, leaning into him with an almost humiliating desperation, wanting to taste him again. To be kissed again. By Joshua Grayson, the man she was committing an insane kind of fraud with. The man who had hired her to play the part of his pretend fiancée.

"That will do," he said, lifting his hand and squeezing her chin gently, those blue eyes glinting with a sharpness that cut straight to her soul. "Yes, Ms. Kelly, that will do quite nicely."

* * *

Claim Me, Cowboy is part of the **Copper Ridge** series from *New York Times* bestselling author Maisey Yates

Dear Reader,

I read a news story about a man who decided to find his son a wife by placing an ad for him in the paper. And of course, I thought, there's a book in that.

It turned out there wasn't just one book in that, but a few.

This particular story starts off with an ad placed by a well-meaning and meddling father. Joshua Grayson's father thinks his son would be happier if he had a wife. Joshua disagrees. And so he places a counter ad of his own, looking for an unsuitable woman to pose as his prospective fiancée, in order to teach his dad a lesson.

But what he gets is a whole lot more than he bargained for.

Love can come from the most unexpected places, and Danielle Kelly and the baby she brings along with her to Joshua's house are definitely unexpected. Definitely unsuitable.

And undoubtedly everything the confirmed bachelor needs.

This book is proof that story inspiration can come from a variety of places. I had fun writing it, and I hope you enjoy it, too.

Happy reading!

Maisey

MAISEY YATES

—

CLAIM ME, COWBOY

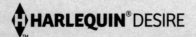
HARLEQUIN® DESIRE

Recycling programs
for this product may
not exist in your area.

ISBN-13: 978-1-335-97141-8

Claim Me, Cowboy

Copyright © 2018 by Maisey Yates

Printed in U.S.A.

Maisey Yates is a *New York Times* bestselling author of more than thirty romance novels. She has a coffee habit she has no interest in kicking and a slight Pinterest addiction. She lives with her husband and children in the Pacific Northwest. When Maisey isn't writing, she can be found singing in the grocery store, shopping for shoes online and probably not doing dishes. Check out her website: maiseyyates.com.

Visit her Author Profile page on Harlequin.com, or maiseyyates.com, for more titles!

For Jackie Ashenden, my conflict guru
and dear friend. Without you my books would
take a heck of a lot longer to write, and my life
would be a heck of a lot more boring.
Thank you for everything. Always.

November 1, 2017
LOOKING FOR A WIFE—

Wealthy bachelor, 34, looking for a wife. Never married, no children. Needs a partner who can attend business and social events around the world. Must be willing to move to Copper Ridge, Oregon. Perks include: travel, an allowance, residence in several multimillion-dollar homes.

November 5, 2017
LOOKING FOR AN UNSUITABLE WIFE—

Wealthy bachelor, 34, irritated, looking for a woman to pretend to be my fiancée in order to teach my meddling father a lesson. Need a partner who is rough around the edges. Must be willing to come to Copper Ridge, Oregon, for at least thirty days. Generous compensation provided.

One

"No. You do not need to *send pics*."

Joshua Grayson looked out the window of his office and did not feel the kind of calm he ought to feel.

He'd moved back to Copper Ridge six months ago from Seattle, happily trading in a man-made, rectangular skyline for the natural curve of the mountains.

Not the best thing for an architect to feel, perhaps. But he spent his working hours dealing in design, in business. Numbers. Black, white and the bottom line. There was something about looking out at the mountains that restarted him.

That, and getting on the back of a horse. Riding from one end of the property to the other. The wind blocking out every other sound except hoofbeats on the earth.

Right now, he doubted anything would decrease the tension he was feeling from dealing with the fallout of his father's ridiculous ad. Another attempt by the old man to make Joshua live the life his father wanted him to.

The only kind of life his father considered successful: a wife, children.

He couldn't understand why Joshua didn't want the same.

No. That kind of life was for another man, one with another past and another future. It was not for Joshua. And that was why he was going to teach his father a lesson.

But not with Brindy, who wanted to send him selfies with "no filter."

The sound she made in response to his refusal was so petulant he almost laughed.

"But your ad said…"

"That," he said, "was not my ad. Goodbye."

He wasn't responsible for the ad in a national paper asking for a wife, till death do them part. But an unsuitable, temporary wife? Yes. That had been his ad.

He was done with his father's machinations. No matter how well-meaning they were. He was tired of tripping over daughters of "old friends" at family gatherings. Tired of dodging women who had been set on him like hounds at a fox hunt.

He was going to win the game. Once and for all. And the woman he hoped would be his trump card was on her way.

His first respondent to his counter ad—Danielle Kelly—was twenty-two, which suited his purposes nicely. His dad would think she was too young, and frankly, Joshua also thought she was too young. He didn't get off on that kind of thing.

He understood why some men did. A tight body was hot. But in his experience, the younger the woman, the less in touch with her sensuality she was and he didn't have the patience for that.

He didn't have the patience for this either, but here he was. The sooner he got this farce over with, the sooner he could go back to his real life.

The doorbell rang and he stood up behind his desk. She was here. And she was—he checked his watch—late.

A half smile curved his lips.

Perfect.

He took the stairs two at a time. He was impatient to meet his temporary bride. Impatient to get this plan started so it could end.

He strode across the entryway and jerked the door open. And froze.

The woman standing on his porch was small.

And young, just as he'd expected, but... She wore no makeup, which made her look like a damned teenager. Her features were fine and pointed; her dark brown hair hung lank beneath a ragged beanie that looked like it was in the process of unraveling while it sat on her head.

He didn't bother to linger over the rest of the details—her threadbare sweater with too-long sleeves, her tragic skinny jeans—because he was stopped, immobilized really, by the tiny bundle in her arms.

A baby.

His prospective bride had come with a baby.

Well, hell.

She really hoped he wasn't a serial killer. Well, *hoped* was an anemic word for what she was feeling. Particularly considering the possibility was a valid concern.

What idiot put an ad in the paper looking for a temporary wife?

Though, she supposed the bigger question was: What idiot responded to an ad in the paper looking for a temporary wife?

This idiot, apparently.

It took Danielle a moment to realize she was staring directly at the center of a broad, muscular male chest. She had to raise her head slightly to see his face. He was just so...tall. And handsome.

And she was confused.

She hadn't imagined that a man who put an ad in the paper for a fake fiancée might be attractive. Another anemic word. *Attractive.* This man wasn't simply *attractive…*

He was… Well, he was unreal.

Broad shouldered, muscular, with stubble on his square jaw adding a roughness to features that might have otherwise been considered pretty.

"Please don't tell me you're Danielle Kelly," he said, crossing his arms over that previously noted broad chest.

"I am. Were you expecting someone else? Of course, I suppose you could be. I bet I'm not the only person who responded to your ad, strange though it was. The mention of compensation was pretty tempting. Although, I might point out that in the future maybe you should space your appointments further apart."

"You have a baby," he said, stating the obvious.

Danielle looked down at the bundle in her arms. "Yes."

"You didn't mention that in our email correspondence."

"Of course not. I thought it would make it too easy for you to turn me away."

He laughed, somewhat reluctantly, a muscle in his jaw twitching. "Well, you're right about that."

"But now I'm here. And I don't have the gas

money to get back home. Also, you said you wanted unsuitable." She spread one arm wide, keeping Riley clutched firmly in her other arm. "I would say that I'm pretty unsuitable."

She could imagine the picture she made. Her hideous, patchwork car parked in the background. Maroon with lighter patches of red and a door that was green, since it had been replaced after some accident that had happened before the car had come into her possession. Then there was her. In all her faded glory. She was hungry, and she knew she'd lost a lot of weight over the past few weeks, which had taken her frame from slim to downright pointy. The circles under her eyes were so dark she almost looked like she'd been punched.

She considered the baby a perfect accessory. She had that new baby sallowness they never told you about when they talked about the miracle of life.

She curled her toes inside her boots, one of them going through a hole at the end of her sock. She frowned. "Anyway, I figured I presented a pretty poor picture of a fiancée for a businessman such as yourself. Don't you agree?"

The corners of his lips tightened further. "The baby."

"Yes?"

"You expect it to live here?"

She made an exasperated noise. "No. I expect

him to live in the car while I party it up in your fancy-pants house."

"A baby wasn't part of the deal."

"What do you care? Your email said it's only through Christmas. Can you imagine telling your father that you've elected to marry Portland hipster trash and she comes with a baby? I mean, it's going to be incredibly awkward, but ultimately kind of funny."

"Come in," he said, his expression no less taciturn as he stood to the side and allowed her entry into his magnificent home.

She clutched Riley even more tightly to her chest as she wandered inside, looking up at the high ceiling, the incredible floor-to-ceiling windows that offered an unparalleled mountain view. As cities went, Portland was all right. The air was pretty clean, and once you got away from the highrise buildings, you could see past the iron and steel to the nature beyond.

But this view… This was something else entirely.

She looked down at the floor, taking a surprised step to the side when she realized she was standing on glass. And that underneath the glass was a small, slow-moving stream. Startlingly clear, rocks visible beneath the surface of the water. Also, fish.

She looked up to see him staring at her. "My sister's work," he said. "She's the hottest new architect on the scene. Incredible, considering she's only in her early twenties. And a woman, breaking serious barriers in the industry."

"That sounds like an excerpt from a magazine article."

He laughed. "It might be. Since I write the press releases about Faith. That's what I do. PR for our firm, which has expanded recently. Not just design, but construction. And as you can see, Faith's work is highly specialized, and it's extremely coveted."

A small prickle of…something worked its way under her skin. She couldn't imagine being so successful at such a young age. Of course, Joshua and his sister must have come from money. You couldn't build something like this if you hadn't.

Danielle was in her early twenties and didn't even have a checking account, much less a successful business.

All of that had to change. It had to change for Riley.

He was why she was here, after all.

Truly, nothing else could have spurred her to answer the ad. She had lived in poverty all of her life. But Riley deserved better. He deserved stability. And he certainly didn't deserve to wind up in foster care just because she couldn't get herself together.

"So," she said, cautiously stepping off the glass

tile. "Tell me more about this situation. And exactly what you expect."

She wanted him to lay it all out. Wanted to hear the terms and conditions he hadn't shared over email. She was prepared to walk away if it was something she couldn't handle. And if he wasn't willing to take no for an answer? Well, she had a knife in her boot.

"My father placed an ad in a national paper saying I was looking for a wife. You can imagine my surprise when I began getting responses before I had ever seen the ad. My father is well-meaning, Ms. Kelly, and he's willing to do anything to make his children's lives better. However, what he perceives as perfection can only come one way. He doesn't think all of this can possibly make me happy." Joshua looked up, seeming to indicate the beautiful house and view around them. "He's wrong. However, he won't take no for an answer, and I want to teach him a lesson."

"By making him think he won?"

"Kind of. That's where you come in. As I said, he can only see things from his perspective. From his point of view, a wife will stay at home and massage my feet while I work to bring in income. He wants someone traditional. Someone soft and biddable." He looked her over. "I imagine you are none of those things."

"Yeah. Not so much." The life she had lived didn't leave room for that kind of softness.

"And you are right. He isn't going to love that you come with a baby. In fact, he'll probably think you're a gold digger."

"I am a gold digger," she said. "If you weren't offering money, I wouldn't be here. I need money, Mr. Grayson, not a fiancé."

"Call me Joshua," he said. "Come with me."

She followed him as he walked through the entryway, through the living area—which looked like something out of a magazine that she had flipped through at the doctor's office once—and into the kitchen.

The kitchen made her jaw drop. Everything was so shiny. Stainless steel surrounded by touches of wood. A strange clash of modern and rustic that seemed to work.

Danielle had never been in a place where so much work had gone into the details. Before Riley, when she had still been living with her mother, the home decor had included plastic flowers shoved into some kind of strange green Styrofoam and a rug in the kitchen that was actually a towel laid across a spot in the linoleum that had been worn through.

"You will live here for the duration of our arrangement. You will attend family gatherings and work events with me."

"Aren't you worried about me being unsuitable for your work arrangements too?"

"Not really. People who do business with us are fascinated by the nontraditional. As I mentioned earlier, my sister, Faith, is something of a pioneer in her field."

"Great," Danielle said, giving him a thumbs-up. "I'm glad to be a nontraditional asset to you."

"Whether or not you're happy with it isn't really my concern. I mean, I'm paying you, so you don't need to be happy."

She frowned. "Well, I don't want to be unhappy. That's the other thing. We have to discuss…terms and stuff. I don't know what all you think you're going to get out of me, but I'm not here to have sex with you. I'm just here to pose as your fiancée. Like the ad said."

The expression on his face was so disdainful it was almost funny. Almost. It didn't quite ascend to funny because it punched her in the ego. "I think I can control myself, Ms. Kelly."

"If I can call you Joshua, then you can call me Danielle," she said.

"Noted."

The way he said it made her think he wasn't necessarily going to comply with her wishes just because she had made them known. He was difficult. No wonder he didn't have an actual woman hanging around willing to marry him. She should have known there was something wrong with him. Because he was rich and kind of disgustingly handsome. His father shouldn't have had to put an ad in the paper to find Joshua a woman.

He should be able to snap his fingers and have them come running.

That sent another shiver of disquiet over her. Yeah, maybe she should listen to those shivers… But the compensation. She needed the compensation.

"What am I going to do…with the rest of my time?"

"Stay here," he said, as though that were the most obvious thing in the world. As though the idea of her rotting away up here in his mansion wasn't weird at all. "And you have that baby. I assume it takes up a lot of your time?"

"He. Riley. And yes, he does take up a lot of time. He's a baby. That's kind of their thing." He didn't respond to that. "You know. Helpless, requiring every single one of their physical and emotional needs to be met by another person. Clearly you don't know."

Something in his face hardened. "No."

"Well, this place is big enough you shouldn't have to ever find out."

"I keep strange hours," he said. "I have to work with offices overseas, and I need to be available to speak to them on the phone, which means I only sleep for a couple of hours at a time. I also spend a lot of time outdoors."

Looking at him, that last statement actually made sense. Yes, he had the bearing of an uptight businessman, but he was wearing a T-shirt and jeans. He was also the kind of physically fit that didn't look like it had come from a gym, not that she was an expert on men or their physiques.

"What's the catch?" she asked.

Nothing in life came this easy—she knew that for certain. She was waiting for the other shoe to drop. Waiting for him to lead her down to the dungeon and show her where he kept his torture pit.

"There is no catch. This is what happens when a man with a perverse sense of humor and too much money decides to teach his father a lesson."

"So basically I live in this beautiful house, I wear your ring, I meet your family, I behave abominably and then I get paid?"

"That is the agreement, Ms. Kelly."

"What if I steal your silverware?"

He chuckled. "Then I still win. If you take off in the dead of night, you don't get your money, and I have the benefit of saying to my father that because of his ad I ended up with a con woman and then got my heart broken."

He really had thought of everything. She supposed there was a reason he was successful.

"So do we... Is this happening?"

"There will be papers for you to sign, but yes. It is." Any uncertainty he'd seemed to feel because of Riley was gone now.

He reached into the pocket of his jeans and pulled out a small, velvet box. He opened it, revealing a diamond ring so beautiful, so big, it bordered on obscene.

This was the moment. This was the moment when he would say he actually needed her to spend the day wandering around dressed as a teddy bear or something.

But that moment didn't come either. Instead, he took the ring out of the box and held it out to her. "Give me your hand."

She complied. She complied before she gave her body permission to. She didn't know what she expected. For him to get down on one knee? For him to slide the ring onto her fourth finger? He did neither. Instead, he dropped the gem into her palm.

She curled her fingers around it, an electric shock moving through her system as she realized she was probably holding more money in her hand right now than she could ever hope to earn over the course of her lifetime.

Well, no, that wasn't true. Because she was about to earn enough money over the next month to take care of herself and Riley forever. To make sure she got permanent custody of him.

Her life had been so hard, a constant series

of moves and increasingly unsavory *uncles* her mother brought in and out of their lives. Hunger, cold, fear, uncertainty...

She wasn't going to let Riley suffer the same fate. No, she was going to make sure her half brother was protected. This agreement, even if Joshua did ultimately want her to walk around dressed like a sexy teddy bear, was a small price to pay for Riley's future.

"Yes," she said, testing the weight of the ring. "It is."

Two

As Joshua followed Danielle down the hall, he regretted not having a live-in housekeeper. An elderly British woman would come in handy at a time like this. She would probably find Danielle and her baby to be absolutely delightful. He, on the other hand, did not.

No, on the contrary, he felt invaded. Which was stupid. Because he had signed on for this. Though, he had signed on for it only after he had seen his father's ad. After he had decided the old man needed to be taught a lesson once and for all about meddling in Joshua's life.

It didn't matter that his father had a soft heart

or that he was coming from a good place. No, what mattered was the fact that Joshua was tired of being hounded every holiday, every time he went to dinner with his parents, about the possibility of him starting a family.

It wasn't going to happen.

At one time, he'd thought that would be his future. Had been looking forward to it. But the people who said it was better to have loved and lost than never to have loved at all clearly hadn't *caused* the loss.

He was happy enough now to be alone. And when he didn't want to be alone, he called a woman, had her come spend a few hours in his bed—or in the back of his truck, he wasn't particular. Love was not on his agenda.

"This is a big house," she said.

Danielle sounded vaguely judgmental, which seemed wrong, all things considered. Sure, he was the guy who had paid a woman to pose as his temporary fiancée. And sure, he was the man who lived in a house that had more square footage than he generally walked through in a day, but she was the one who had responded to an ad placed by a complete stranger looking for a temporary fiancée. So, all things considered, he didn't feel like she had a lot of room to judge.

"Yes, it is."

"Why? I mean, you live here alone, right?"

"Because size matters," he said, ignoring the shifting, whimpering sound of the baby in her arms.

"Right," she said, her tone dry. "I've lived in apartment buildings that were smaller than this."

He stopped walking, then he turned to face her. "Am I supposed to feel something about that? Feel sorry for you? Feel bad about the fact that I live in a big house? Because trust me, I started humbly enough. I choose to live differently than my parents. Because I can. Because I earned it."

"Oh, I see. In that case, I suppose I earned my dire straits."

"I don't know your life, Danielle. More important, I don't want to know it." He realized that was the first time he had used her first name. He didn't much care.

"Great. Same goes. Except I'm going to be living in your house, so I'm going to definitely…infer some things about your life. And that might give rise to conversations like this one. And if you're going to be assuming things about me, then you should be prepared for me to respond in kind."

"I don't have to do any such thing. As far as I'm concerned, I'm the employer, you're the employee. That means if I want to talk to you about the emotional scars of my childhood, you had better lie back on my couch and listen. Conversely, if I do not want to hear about any of the scars of yours, I don't have to. All I have to do is throw money at you until you stop talking."

"Wow. It's seriously the job offer I've been waiting for my entire life. Talking I'm pretty good at. And I don't do a great job of shutting up. That means I would be getting money thrown at me for a long, long time."

"Don't test me, Ms. Kelly," he said, reverting back to her last name, because he really didn't want to know about her childhood or what brought her here. Didn't want to wonder about her past. Didn't want to wonder about her adulthood either. Who the father of her baby was. What kind of situation she was in. It wasn't his business, and he didn't care.

"Don't test me, Ms. Kelly," she said, in what he assumed was supposed to be a facsimile of his voice.

"Really?" he asked.

"What? You can't honestly expect to operate at this level of extreme douchiness and not get called to the carpet on it."

"I expect that I can do whatever I want, since I'm paying you to be here."

"You don't want me to dress up as a teddy bear and vacuum, do you?"

"What?"

She shifted her weight, moving the baby over to one hip and spreading the other arm wide. "Hey, man, some people are into that. They like stuffed animals. Or rather, they like people dressed as stuffed animals."

"I don't."

"That's a relief."

"I like women," he said. "Dressed as women. Or rather, undressed, generally."

"I'm not judging. Your dad put an ad in the paper for some reason. Clearly he really wants you to be married."

"Yes. Well, he doesn't understand that not everybody needs to live the life that he does. He was happy with a family and a farmhouse. But none of the rest of us feel that way, and there's nothing wrong with that."

"So none of you are married?"

"One of us is. The only brother that actually wanted a farmhouse too." He paused in front of the door at the end of the hall. He was glad he had decided to set this room aside for the woman who answered the ad. He hadn't known she would come with a baby in tow, but the fact that she had meant he really, really wanted her out of earshot.

"Is this it?" she asked.

"Yes," he said, pushing the door open.

When she looked inside the bedroom, her jaw dropped, and Joshua couldn't deny that he took a small amount of satisfaction in her reaction. She looked… Well, she looked amazed. Like somebody standing in front of a great work of art. Except it was just a bedroom. Rather a grand one, he had to admit, down to the details.

There was a large bed fashioned out of natural, twisted pieces of wood with polished support beams that ran from floor to ceiling and retained the natural shape they'd had in the woods but glowed from the stain that had been applied to them. The bed made the whole room look like a magical forest. A little bit fanciful for him. His own bedroom had been left more Spartan. But, clearly, Danielle was enchanted.

And he shouldn't care.

"I've definitely lived in apartments that were smaller than this room," she said, wrapping both arms around the baby and turning in a circle. "This is… Is that a loft? Like a reading loft?" She was gazing up at the mezzanine designed to look as though it was nestled in the tree branches.

"I don't know." He figured it was probably more of a sex loft. But then, if he slept in a room with a loft, obviously he would have sex in it. That was what creative surfaces were for, in his opinion.

"It reminds me of something we had when I was in first grade." A crease appeared between her eyebrows. "I mean, not me as in at our house, but in my first-grade classroom at school. The teacher really loved books. And she liked for us all to read. So we were able to lie around the class-

room anywhere we wanted with a book and—"
She abruptly stopped talking, as though she realized exactly what she was doing. "Never mind.
You think it's boring. Anyway, I'm going to use
it for a reading loft."

"Dress like a teddy bear in it, for all I care," he
responded.

"That's your thing, not mine."

"Do you have any bags in the car that I can get
for you?"

She looked genuinely stunned. "You don't have
to get anything for me."

It struck him that she thought he was being nice.
He didn't consider the offer particularly nice. It was
just what his father had drilled into him from the
time he was a boy. If there was a woman and she
had a heavy thing to transport, you were no kind
of man if you didn't offer to do the transporting.

"I don't mind."

"It's just one bag," she said.

That shocked him. She was a woman. A woman
with a baby. He was pretty sure most mothers trav-
eled with enough luggage to fill a caravan. "Just
one bag." He had to confirm that.

"Yes," she returned. "Baggage is another thing
entirely. But in terms of bags, yeah, we travel
light."

"Let me get it." He turned and walked out of

the room, frustrated when he heard her footsteps behind him. "I said I would get it."

"You don't need to," she said, following him persistently down the stairs and out toward the front door.

"My car is locked," she added, and he ignored her as he continued to walk across the driveway to the maroon monstrosity parked there.

He shot her a sideways glance, then looked down at the car door. It hung a little bit crooked, and he lifted up on it hard enough to push it straight, then he jerked it open. "Not well."

"You're the worst," she said, scowling.

He reached into the back seat and saw one threadbare duffel bag, which had to be the bag she was talking about. The fabric strap was dingy, and he had a feeling it used to be powder blue. The zipper was broken and there were four safety pins holding the end of the bulging bag together. All in all, it looked completely impractical.

"Empty all the contents out of this tonight. In the morning, I'm going to use it to fuel a bonfire."

"It's the only bag I have."

"I'll buy you a new one."

"It better be in addition to the fee that I'm getting," she said, her expression stubborn. "I mean it. If I incur a loss because of you, you better cover it."

"You have my word that if anything needs to be purchased in order for you to fit in with your surroundings, or in order for me to avoid contracting scabies, it will be bankrolled by me."

"I don't have scabies," she said, looking fierce.

"I didn't say you did. I implied that your gym bag might."

"Well," she said, her cheeks turning red, "it doesn't. It's clean. I'm clean."

He heaved the bag over his shoulder and led the way back to the house, Danielle trailing behind him like an angry wood nymph. That was what she reminded him of, he decided. All pointed angles and spiky intensity. And a supernaturally wicked glare that he could feel boring into the center of his back. Right between his shoulder blades.

This was not a woman who intimidated easily, if at all.

He supposed that was signal enough that he should make an attempt to handle her with care. Not because she needed it, but because clearly nobody had ever made the attempt before. But he didn't know how. And he was paying her an awful lot to put up with him as he was.

And she had brought a baby into his house.

"You're going to need some supplies," he said, frowning. Because he abruptly realized what it meant that she had brought a baby into his house. The bedroom he had installed her in was only meant for one. And there was no way—barring the unlikely reality that she was related to Mary

Poppins in some way—that her ratty old bag contained the supplies required to keep both a baby and herself in the kind of comfort that normal human beings expected.

"What kind of supplies?"

He moved quickly through the house, and she scurried behind him, attempting to match his steps. They walked back into the bedroom and he flung the bag on the ground.

"A bed for the baby. Beyond that, I don't know what they require."

She shot him a deadly glare, then bent down and unzipped the bag, pulling out a bottle and a can of formula. She tossed both onto the bed, then reached back into the bag and grabbed a blanket. She spread it out on the floor, then set the baby in the center of it.

Then she straightened, spreading her arms wide and slapping her hands back down on her thighs. "Well, this is more than we've had for a long time. And yeah, I guess it would be nice to have nursery stuff. But I've never had it. Riley and I have been doing just fine on our own." She looked down, picking at some dirt beneath her fingernail. "Or I guess we haven't been *fine*. If we had, I wouldn't have responded to your ad. But I don't need more than what I have. Not now. Once you pay me? Well, I'm going to buy a house. I'm going to change things for us. But until then, it doesn't matter."

He frowned. "What about Riley's father? Surely he should be paying you some kind of support."

"Right. Like I have any idea who he is." He must have made some kind of facial expression that seemed judgmental, because her face colored and her eyebrows lowered. "I mean, I don't know how to get in touch with him. It's not like he left contact details. And I sincerely doubt he left his real name."

"I'll call our office assistant, Poppy. She'll probably know what you need." Technically, Poppy was his brother Isaiah's assistant, but she often handled whatever Joshua or Faith needed, as well. Poppy would arrange it so that various supplies were overnighted to the house.

"Seriously. Don't do anything... You don't need to do anything."

"I'm supposed to convince my parents that I'm marrying you," he said, his tone hard. "I don't think they're going to believe I'm allowing my fiancée to live out of one duffel bag. No. Everything will have to be outfitted so that it looks legitimate. Consider it a bonus to your salary."

She tilted her chin upward, her eyes glittering. "Okay, I will."

He had halfway expected her to argue, but he wasn't sure why. She was here for her own material gain. Why would she reduce it? "Good." He nodded once. "You probably won't see much of me. I'll be working a lot. We are going to have dinner with my parents in a couple of days. Until then, the house and the property are yours to explore. This is your house too. For the time being."

He wasn't being particularly generous. It was just that he didn't want to answer questions, or deal with her being tentative about where she might and might not be allowed to go. He just wanted to install her and the baby in this room and forget about them until he needed them as convenient props.

"Really?" Her natural suspicion was shining through again.

"I'm a very busy man, Ms. Kelly," he said. "I'm not going to be babysitting. Either the child or you."

And with that, he turned and left her alone.

Three

Danielle had slept fitfully last night. And, of course, she hadn't actually left her room once she had been put there. But early the next morning there had been a delivery. And the signature they had asked for was hers. And then the packages had started to come in, like a Christmas parade without the wrapping.

Teams of men carried the boxes up the stairs. They had assembled a crib, a chair, and then unpacked various baby accoutrements that Danielle hadn't even known existed. How could she? She certainly hadn't expected to end up caring for a baby.

When her mother had breezed back into her life alone and pregnant—after Danielle had experienced just two carefree years where she had her own space and wasn't caring for anyone—Danielle had put all of her focus into caring for the other woman. Into arranging state health insurance so the prenatal care and hospital bill for the delivery wouldn't deter her mother from actually taking care of herself and the baby.

And then, when her mother had abandoned Danielle and Riley...that was when Danielle had realized her brother was likely going to be her responsibility. She had involved Child Services not long after that.

There had been two choices. Either Riley could go into foster care or Danielle could take some appropriate parenting classes and become a temporary guardian.

So she had.

But she had been struggling to keep their heads above water, and it was too close to the way she had grown up. She wanted more than that for Riley. Wanted more than that for both of them. Now it wasn't just her. It was him. And a part-time job as a cashier had never been all that lucrative. But with Riley to take care of, and her mother completely out of the picture, staying afloat on a cashier's pay was impossible.

She had done her best trading babysitting time

with a woman in her building who also had a baby and nobody else to depend on. But inevitably there were schedule clashes, and after missing a few too many shifts, Danielle had lost her job.

Which was when she had gotten her first warning from Child Services.

Well, she had a job now.

And, apparently, a full nursery.

Joshua was refreshingly nowhere to be seen, which made dealing with her new circumstances much easier. Without him looming over her, being in his house felt a lot like being in the world's fanciest vacation rental. At least, the fanciest vacation rental she could imagine.

She had a baby monitor in her pocket, one that would allow her to hear when Riley woke up. A baby monitor that provided her with more freedom than she'd had since Riley had been born. But, she supposed, in her old apartment a monitor would have been a moot point considering there wasn't anywhere she could go and not hear the baby cry.

But in this massive house, having Riley take his nap in the bedroom—in the new crib, his first crib—would have meant she couldn't have also run down to the kitchen to grab snacks. But she had the baby monitor. A baby monitor that vibrated. Which meant she could also listen to music.

She had the same ancient MP3 player her mother had given her for her sixteenth birthday years ago, but Danielle had learned early to hold on to everything she had, because she didn't know when something else would come along. And in the case of frills like her MP3 player, nothing else had ever come along.

Of course, that meant her music was as old as her technology. But really, music hadn't been as good since she was sixteen anyway.

She shook her hips slightly, walking through the kitchen, singing about how what didn't kill her would only make her stronger. Digging through cabinets, she came up with a package of Pop-Tarts. *Pop-Tarts!*

Her mother had never bought those. They were too expensive. And while Danielle had definitely indulged herself when she had moved out, that hadn't lasted. Because they were too expensive.

Joshua had strawberry. And some kind of mixed berry with bright blue frosting. She decided she would eat one of each to ascertain which was best.

Then she decided to eat one more of each. She hadn't realized how hungry she was. She had a feeling the hunger wasn't a new development. She had a feeling she had been hungry for days. Weeks even.

Suddenly, sitting on the plush couch in his living area, shoving toaster pastries into her mouth, she felt a whole lot like crying in relief. Because she and Riley were warm; they were safe. And there was hope. Finally, an end point in sight to the long, slow grind of poverty she had existed in for her entire life.

It seemed too good to be true, really. That she had managed to jump ahead in her life like this. That she was really managing to get herself out of that hole without prostituting herself.

Okay, so some people might argue this agreement with Joshua *was* prostituting herself, a little bit. But it wasn't like she was going to have sex with him.

She nearly choked on her Pop-Tart at the thought. And she lingered a little too long on what it might be like to get close to a man like Joshua. To any man, really. The way her mother had behaved all of her life had put Danielle off men. Or, more specifically, she supposed it was the way men had behaved toward Danielle's mother that had put her off.

As far as Danielle could tell, relationships were a whole lot of exposing yourself to pain, deciding you were going to depend on somebody and then having that person leave you high and dry.

No, thank you.

But she supposed she could see how somebody might lose their mind enough to take that risk. Especially when the person responsible for the mind loss had eyes that were blue like Joshua's. She leaned back against the couch, her hand falling slack, the Pop-Tart dangling from her fingertips.

Yesterday there had been the faint shadow of golden stubble across that strong face and jaw, his eyes glittering with irritation. Which she supposed shouldn't be a bonus, shouldn't be appealing. Except his irritation made her want to rise to the unspoken challenge. To try to turn that spark into something else. Turn that irritation into something more...

"Are you eating my Pop-Tarts?"

The voice cut through the music and she jumped, flinging the toaster pastry into the air. She ripped her headphones out of her ears and turned around to see Joshua, his arms crossed over his broad chest, his eyebrows flat on his forehead, his expression unreadable.

"You said whatever was in your house was mine to use," she squeaked. "And a warning would've been good. You just about made me jump out of my skin. Which was maybe your plan all along. If you wanted to make me into a skin suit."

"That's ridiculous. I would not fit into your skin."

She swallowed hard, her throat dry. "Well, it's a figure of speech, isn't it?"

"Is it?" he asked.

"Yes. Everybody knows what that means. It means that I think you might be a serial killer."

"You don't really think I'm a serial killer, or you wouldn't be here."

"I am pretty desperate." She lifted her hand and licked off a remnant of jam. "I mean, obviously."

"There are no Pop-Tarts left," he said, his tone filled with annoyance.

"You said I could have whatever I wanted. I wanted Pop-Tarts."

"You ate all of them."

"Why do you even have Pop-Tarts?" She stood up, crossing her arms, mimicking his stance. "You don't look like a man who eats Pop-Tarts."

"I like them. I like to eat them after I work outside."

"You work outside?"

"Yes," he said. "I have horses."

Suddenly, all of her annoyance fell away. Like it had been melted by magic. *Equine* magic. "You have horses?" She tried to keep the awe out of her voice, but it was nearly impossible.

"Yes," he said.

"Can I... Can I see them?"

"If you want to."

She had checked the range on the baby monitor, so depending on how far away from the house the horses were, she could go while Riley was napping.

"Could we see the house from the barn? Or wherever you keep them?"

"Yeah," he said, "it's just right across the drive-way."

"Can I see them *now*?"

"I don't know. You ate my Pop-Tarts. Actually, more egregious than eating my Pop-Tarts, you threw the last half of one on the ground."

"Sorry about your Pop-Tarts. But I'm sure that a man who can have an entire nursery outfitted in less than twenty-four hours can certainly acquire Pop-Tarts at a moment's notice."

"Or I could just go to the store."

She had a hard time picturing a man like Joshua Grayson walking through the grocery store. In fact, the image almost made her laugh. He was way too commanding to do something as mundane as pick up a head of lettuce and try to figure out how fresh it was. Far too…masculine to go around squeezing avocados.

"What?" he asked, his eyebrows drawing together.

"I just can't imagine you going to the grocery store. That's all."

"Well, I do. Because I like food. Food like Pop-Tarts."

"My mom would never buy those for me," she said. "They were too expensive."

He huffed out a laugh. "My mom would never buy them for me."

"This is why being an adult is cool, even when it sucks."

"Pop-Tarts whenever you want?"

She nodded. "Yep."

"That seems like a low bar."

She lifted a shoulder. "Maybe it is, but it's a tasty one."

He nodded. "Fair enough. Now, why don't we go look at the horses."

Joshua didn't know what to expect by taking Danielle outside to see the horses. He had been irritated that she had eaten his preferred afternoon snack, and then, perversely, even more irritated that she had questioned the fact that it was his preferred afternoon snack. Irritated that he was put in the position of explaining to someone what he did with his time and what he put into his body.

He didn't like explaining himself.

But then she saw the horses. And all his irritation faded as he took in the look on her face. She was filled with...wonder. Absolute wonder over this thing he took for granted.

The fact that he owned horses at all, that he had felt compelled to acquire some once he had moved into this place, was a source of consternation. He had hated doing farm chores when he was a kid. Hadn't been able to get away from home and to the city fast enough. But in recent years, those feelings had started to change. And he'd found himself seeking out roots. Seeking out home.

For better or worse, this was home. Not just the misty Oregon coast, not just the town of Copper Ridge. But a ranch. Horses. A morning spent riding until the sun rose over the mountains, washing everything in a pale gold.

Yeah, that was home.

He could tell this ranch he loved was something beyond a temporary home for Danielle, who was looking at the horses and the barn like they were magical things.

She wasn't wearing her beanie today. Her dark brown hair hung limply around her face. She was pale, her chin pointed, her nose slightly pointed, as well. She was elfin, and he wasn't tempted to call her beautiful, but there was something captivating about her. Something fascinating. Watching her with the large animals was somehow just as entertaining as watching football and he couldn't quite figure out why.

"You didn't grow up around horses?"

"No," she said, taking a timid step toward the paddock. "I grew up in Portland."

He nodded. "Right."

"Always in apartments," she said. Then she frowned. "I think one time we had a house. I can't really remember it. We moved a lot. But sometimes when we lived with my mom's boyfriends, we had nicer places. It had its perks."

"What did?"

"My mom being a codependent hussy," she said, her voice toneless so it was impossible to say whether or not she was teasing.

"Right." He had grown up in one house. His family had never moved. His parents were still in that same farmhouse, the one his family had owned for a couple of generations. He had moved away to go to college and then to start the business, but that was different. He had always known he could come back here. He'd always had roots.

"Will you go back to Portland when you're finished here?" he asked.

"I don't know," she said, blinking rapidly. "I've never really had a choice before. Of where I wanted to live."

It struck him then that she was awfully young. And that he didn't know quite *how* young. "You're twenty-two?"

"Yes," she said, sounding almost defensive. "So I haven't really had a chance to think about what all I want to do and, like, be. When I grow up and stuff."

"Right," he said.

He'd been aimless for a while, but before he'd graduated high school, he'd decided he couldn't deal with a life of ranching in Copper Ridge. He had decided to get out of town. He had wanted more. He had wanted bigger. He'd gone to school for marketing because he was good at selling ideas. Products. He wasn't necessarily the one who created them, or the one who dreamed them up, but he was the one who made sure a consumer would see them and realize that product was what their life had been missing up until that point.

He was the one who took the straw and made it into gold.

He had always enjoyed his job, but it would have been especially satisfying if he'd been able to start his career by building a business with his brother and sister. To be able to market Faith's extraordinary talent to the world, as he did now. But he wasn't sure that he'd started out with a passion for what he did so much as a passion for wealth and success, and that had meant leaving behind his sister and brother too, at first. But his career had certainly grown into a passion. And he'd learned that he was the practical piece. The part that everybody needed.

A lot of people had ideas, but less than half of them had the follow-through to complete what they started. And less than half of *those* people knew how to get to the consumer. That was where he came in.

He'd had his first corporate internship at the

age of twenty. He couldn't imagine being aimless at twenty-two.

But then, Danielle had a baby and he couldn't imagine having a baby at that age either.

A hollow pang struck him in the chest.

He didn't like thinking of babies at all.

"You're judging me," she said, taking a step back from the paddock.

"No, I'm not. Also, you can get closer. You can pet them."

Her head whipped around to look at the horses, then back to him, her eyes round and almost comically hopeful. "I can?"

"Of course you can. They don't bite. Well, they *might* bite, just don't stick your fingers in their mouths."

"I don't know," she said, stuffing her hands in her pockets. Except he could tell she really wanted to. She was just afraid.

"Danielle," he said, earning himself a shocked look when he used her name. "Pet the horses."

She tugged her hand out of her pocket again, then took a tentative step forward, reaching out, then drawing her hand back just as quickly.

He couldn't stand it. Between her not knowing what she wanted to be when she grew up and watching her struggle with touching a horse, he just couldn't deal with it. He stepped forward, wrapped his fingers around her wrist and drew her closer to the paddock. "It's fine," he said.

A moment after he said the words, his body registered what he had done. More than that, it registered the fact that she was very warm. That her skin was smooth.

And that she was way, way too thin.

A strange combination of feelings tightened his whole body. Compassion tightened his heart; lust tightened his groin.

He gritted his teeth. "Come on," he said.

He noticed the color rise in her face, and he wondered if she was angry, or if she was feeling the same flash of awareness rocking through him. He supposed it didn't matter either way. "Come on," he said, drawing her hand closer to the opening of the paddock. "There you go, hold your hand flat like that."

She complied, and he released his hold on her, taking a step back. He did his best to ignore the fact that he could still feel the impression of her skin against his palm.

One of his horses—a gray mare named Blue— walked up to the bars and pressed her nose against Danielle's outstretched hand. Danielle made a sharp, shocked sound, drew her hand back, then giggled. "Her whiskers are soft."

"Yeah," he said, a smile tugging at his lips.

"And she is about as gentle as they come, so you don't have to be afraid of her."

"I'm not afraid of anything," Danielle said, sticking her hand back in, letting the horse sniff her.

He didn't believe that she wasn't afraid of anything. She was definitely tough. But she was brittle. Like one of those people who might withstand a beating, but if something ever hit a fragile spot, she would shatter entirely.

"Would you like to go riding sometime?" he asked.

She drew her hand back again, her expression… Well, he couldn't quite read it. There was a softness to it, but also an edge of fear and suspicion.

"I don't know. Why?"

"You seem to like the horses."

"I do. But I don't know how to ride."

"I can teach you."

"I don't know. I have to watch Riley." She began to withdraw, both from him and from the paddock.

"I'm going to hire somebody to help watch Riley," he said, making that decision right as the words exited his mouth.

There was that look again. Suspicion. "Why?"

"In case I need you for something that isn't baby friendly. Which will probably happen. We have over a month ahead of us with you living with me, and one never knows what kinds of situations we might run into. I wasn't expecting you to come with a baby, and while I agree that it will definitely help make the case that you're not suitable for me, I also think we'll need to be able to go out without him."

She looked very hesitant about that idea. And he could understand why. She clung to that baby like he was a life preserver. Like if she let go of him, she might sink and be in over her head completely.

"And I would get to ride the horses?" she asked, her eyes narrowed, full of suspicion still.

"I said so."

"Sure. But that doesn't mean a lot to me, Mr. Grayson," she said. "I don't accept people at their word. I like legal documents."

"Well, I'm not going to draw up a legal document about giving you horse-riding lessons. So you're going to have to trust me."

"You want me to trust the sketchy rich dude who put an ad in the paper looking for a fake wife?"

"He's the devil you made the deal with, Ms. Kelly. I would say it's in your best interest to trust him."

"We shake on it at least."

She stuck her hand out, and he could see she was completely sincere. So he stuck his out in kind, wrapping his fingers around hers, marveling at her delicate bone structure. Feeling guilty now about getting angry over her eating his Pop-

Tarts. The woman needed him to hire a gourmet chef too. Needed him to make sure she was getting three meals a day. He wondered how long it had been since she'd eaten regularly. She certainly didn't have the look of a woman who had recently given birth. There was no extra weight on her to speak of. He wondered how she had survived something so taxing as labor and delivery. But those were questions he was not going to ask. They weren't his business.

And he shouldn't even be curious about them.

"All right," she said. "You can hire somebody. And I'll learn to ride horses."

"You're a tough negotiator," he said, releasing his hold on her hand.

"Maybe I should go into business."

He tried to imagine this fragile, spiky creature in a boardroom, and it nearly made him laugh. "If you want to," he said, instead of laughing. Because he had a feeling she might attack him if he made fun of her. And another feeling that if Danielle attacked, she would likely go straight for the eyes. Or the balls.

He was attached to both of those things, and he liked them attached to him.

"I should go back to the house. Riley might wake up soon. Plus, I'm not entirely sure if I trust the new baby monitor. I mean, it's probably fine.

But I'm going to have to get used to it before I really depend on it."

"I understand," he said, even though he didn't.

He turned and walked with her back toward the house. He kept his eyes on her small, determined frame. On the way, she stuffed her hands in her pockets and hunched her shoulders forward. As though she were trying to look intimidating. Trying to keep from looking at her surroundings in case her surroundings looked back.

And then he reminded himself that none of this mattered. She was just a means to an end, even if she was a slightly more multifaceted means than he had thought she might be.

It didn't matter how many facets she had. Danielle Kelly needed to fulfill only one objective. She had to be introduced to his parents and be found completely wanting.

He looked back at her, at her determined walk and her posture that seemed to radiate with *I'll cut you*.

Yeah. He had a feeling she would fulfill that objective just fine.

Four

Danielle was still feeling wobbly after her interaction with Joshua down at the barn. She had touched a horse. And she had touched *him*. She hadn't counted on doing either of those things today. And he had told her they were going to have dinner together tonight and he was going to give her a crash course on the Grayson family. She wasn't entirely sure she felt ready for that either.

She had gone through all her clothes, looking for something suitable for having dinner with a billionaire. She didn't have anything. Obviously.

She snorted, feeling like an idiot for thinking

she could find something relatively appropriate in that bag of hers. A bag he thought had scabies.

She turned her snort into a growl.

Then, rebelliously, she pulled out the same pair of faded pants she had been wearing yesterday.

He had probably never dealt with a woman who wore the same thing twice. Let alone the same thing two days in a row. Perversely, she kind of enjoyed that. Hey, she was here to be unsuitable. Might as well start now.

She looked in the mirror, grabbed one stringy end of her hair and blew out a disgusted breath. She shouldn't care how her hair looked.

But he was just so good-looking. It made her feel like a small, brown mouse standing next to him. It wasn't fair, really. That he had the resources to buy himself nice clothes and that he just naturally looked great.

She sighed, picking Riley up from his crib and sticking him in the little carrier she would put him in for dinner. He was awake and looking around, so she wanted to be in his vicinity, rather than leaving him upstairs alone. He wasn't a fussy baby. Really, he hardly ever cried.

But considering how often his mother had left him alone in those early days of his life, before Danielle had realized she couldn't count on her mother to take good care of him, she was reluctant to leave him by himself unless he was sleeping.

Then she paused, going back over to her bag to get the little red, dog-eared dictionary inside. She bent down, still holding on to Riley, and retrieved it. Then she quickly looked up scabies.

"I knew it," she said derisively, throwing the dictionary back into her bag.

She walked down the stairs and into the dining room, setting Riley in his seat on the chair next to hers. Joshua was already sitting at the table, looking as though he had been waiting for them. Which, she had a feeling, he was doing just to be annoying and superior.

"My bag can't have scabies," she said by way of greeting.

"Oh really?"

"Yes. I looked it up. Scabies are mites that burrow into your skin. Not into a duffel bag."

"They have to come from somewhere."

"Well, they're not coming from my bag. They're more likely to come from your horses, or something."

"You like my horses," he said, his tone dry. "Anyway, we're about to have dinner. So maybe we shouldn't be discussing skin mites?"

"You're the one who brought up scabies. The first time."

"I had pretty much dropped the subject."

"Easy enough for you to do, since it wasn't your hygiene being maligned."

"Sure." He stood up from his position at the table. "I'm just going to go get dinner, since you're here. I had it warming."

"Did you cook?"

He left the room without answering and returned a moment later holding two plates full of hot food. Her stomach growled intensely. She didn't even care what was on the plates. As far as she was concerned, it was gourmet. It was warm and obviously not from a can or a frozen pizza box. Plus, she was sitting at a real dining table and not on a patio set that had been shoved into her tiny living room.

The meal looked surprisingly healthy, considering she had discovered his affinity for Pop-Tarts earlier. And it was accompanied by a particularly nice-looking rice. "What is this?"

"Chicken and risotto," he said.

"What's risotto?"

"Creamy rice," he said. "At least, that's the simple explanation."

Thankfully, he wasn't looking at her like she was an alien for not knowing about risotto. But then she remembered he had spoken of having simple roots. So maybe he was used to dealing with people who didn't have as sophisticated a palate as he had.

She wrinkled her nose, then picked up her fork and took a tentative bite. It was good. So good.

And before she knew it, she had cleared out her portion. Her cheeks heated when she realized he had barely taken two bites.

"There's plenty more in the kitchen," he said. Then he took her plate from in front of her and went back into the kitchen. She was stunned, and all she could do was sit there and wait until he returned a moment later with the entire pot of risotto, another portion already on her plate.

"Eat as much as you want," he said, setting everything in front of her.

Well, she wasn't going to argue with that suggestion. She polished off the chicken, then went back for thirds of the risotto. Eventually, she got around to eating the salad.

"I thought we were going to talk about my responsibilities for being your fiancée and stuff," she said after she realized he had been sitting there staring at her for the past ten minutes.

"I thought you should have a chance to eat a meal first."

"Well," she said, taking another bite, "that's unexpectedly kind of you."

"You seem…hungry."

That was the most loaded statement of the century. She was so hungry. For so many things. Food was kind of the least of it. "It's just been a really crazy few months."

"How old is the baby? Riley. How old is Riley?"

For the first time, because of that correction, she became aware of the fact that he seemed reluctant to call Riley by name. Actually, Joshua seemed pretty reluctant to deal with Riley in general.

Riley was unperturbed. Sitting in that reclined seat, his muddy blue eyes staring up at the ceiling. He lifted his fist, putting it in his mouth and gumming it idly.

That was one good thing she could say about their whole situation. Riley was so young that he was largely unperturbed by all of it. He had gone along more or less unaffected by their mother's mistakes. At least, Danielle hoped so. She really did.

"He's almost four months old," she said. She felt a soft smile touch her lips. Yes, taking care of her half brother was hard. None of it was easy. But he had given her a new kind of purpose. Had given her a kind of the drive she'd been missing before.

Before Riley, she had been somewhat content to just enjoy living life on her own terms. To enjoy not cleaning up her mother's messes. Instead, working at the grocery store, going out with friends after work for coffee or burritos at the twenty-four-hour Mexican restaurant.

Her life had been simple, and it had been carefree. Something she hadn't been afforded all the years she'd lived with her mother, dealing with her mother's various heartbreaks, schemes to try to better their circumstances and intense emotional lows.

So many years when Danielle should have been a child but instead was expected to be the parent. If her mother passed out in the bathroom after having too much to drink, it was up to Danielle to take care of her. To put a pillow underneath her mother's head, then make herself a piece of toast for dinner and get her homework done.

In contrast, taking care of only herself had seemed simple. And in truth, she had resented Riley at first, resented the idea that she would have to take care of another person again. But taking care of a baby was different. He wasn't a victim of his own bad choices. No, he was a victim of circumstances. He hadn't had a chance to make a single choice for himself yet.

To Danielle, Riley was the child she'd once been.

Except she hadn't had anyone to step in and take care of her when her mother failed. But Riley did. That realization had filled Danielle with passion. Drive.

And along with that dedication came a fierce, unexpected love like she had never felt before toward another human being. She would do anything for him. Give anything for him.

"And you've been alone with him all this time?"

She didn't know why she was so reluctant to let

Joshua know that Riley wasn't her son. She supposed it was partly because, for all intents and purposes, he was her son. She intended to adopt him officially as soon as she had the means to do so. As soon as everything in her life was in order enough that Child Services would respond to her favorably.

The other part was that as long as people thought Riley was hers, they would be less likely to suggest she make a different decision about his welfare. Joshua Grayson had a coldness to him. He seemed to have a family who loved and supported him, but instead of finding it endearing, he got angry about it. He was using her to get back at his dad for doing something that, in her opinion, seemed mostly innocuous. And yes, she was benefiting from his pettiness, so she couldn't exactly judge.

Still, she had a feeling that if he knew Riley wasn't her son, he would suggest she do the "responsible" thing and allow him to be raised by a two-parent family, or whatever. She just didn't even want to have that discussion with him. Or with anybody. She had too many things against her already.

She didn't want to fight about this too.

"Mostly," she said carefully, treading the line between the truth and a lie. "Since he was about three weeks old. And I thought… I thought I could do it. I'd been self-sufficient for a long time. But then I realized there are a lot of logistical problems when you can't just leave your apartment whenever you want. It's harder to get to work. And I couldn't afford childcare. There wasn't any space at the places that had subsidized rates. So I was trading childcare with a neighbor, but sometimes our schedules conflicted. Anyway, it was just difficult. You can imagine why responding to your ad seemed like the best possible solution."

"I already told you, I'm not judging you for taking me up on an offer I made."

"I guess I'm just explaining that under other circumstances I probably wouldn't have sought you out. But things have been hard. I lost my job because I wasn't flexible enough and I had missed too many shifts because babysitting for Riley fell through."

"Well," he said, a strange expression crossing his face, "your problems should be minimized soon. You should be independently wealthy enough to at least afford childcare."

Not only that, she would actually be able to make decisions about her life. About what she wanted. When Joshua had asked her earlier today about whether or not she would go back to Portland, it had been the first time she had truly realized she could make decisions about where she wanted to live, rather than just parking herself somewhere because she happened to be there already.

It would be the first time in her life she could make proactive decisions rather than just reacting to her situation.

"Right. So I guess we should talk about your family," she said, determined to move the conversation back in the right direction. She didn't need to talk about herself. They didn't need to get to know each other. She just needed to do this thing, to trick his family, lie...whatever he needed her to do. So she and Riley could start their new life.

"I already told you my younger sister is an architectural genius. My older brother Isaiah is the financial brain. And I do the public relations and marketing. We have another brother named Devlin, and he runs a small ranching operation in town. He's married, no kids. Then there are my parents."

"The reason we find ourselves in this situation," she said, folding her hands and leaning forward. Then she cast a glance at the pot of risotto and decided to grab the spoon and serve herself another helping while they were talking.

"Yes. Well, not my mother so much. Sure, she wrings her hands and looks at me sadly and says she wishes I would get married. My father is the one who...actively meddles."

"That surprises me. I mean, given what I know

about fathers. Which is entirely based on TV. I don't have one."

He lifted a brow.

"Well," she continued, "sure, I guess I do. But I never met him. I mean, I don't even know his name."

She realized that her history was shockingly close to the story she had given about Riley. Which was a true one. It just wasn't about Danielle. It was about her mother. And the fact that her mother repeated the same cycle over and over again. The fact that she never seemed to change. And never would.

"That must've been hard," he said. "I'm sorry."

"Don't apologize. I bet he was an ass. I mean, circumstances would lead you to believe that he must be, right?"

"Yeah, it's probably a pretty safe assumption."

"Well, anyway, this isn't about my lack of a paternal figure. This is about the overbearing presence of yours."

He laughed. "My mother is old-fashioned—so is my father. My brother Devlin is a little bit too, but he's also something of a rebel. He has tattoos and things. He's a likely ally for you, especially since he got married a few months ago and is feeling soft about love and all of that. My brother Isaiah isn't going to like you. My sister, Faith, will try. Basically, if you cuss, chew with your mouth open, put your elbows on the table and in general act like a feral cat, my family will likely find you unsuitable. Also, if you could maybe repeatedly bring up the fact that you're really looking forward to spending my money, and that you had another man's baby four months ago, that would be great."

She squinted. "I think the fact that I have a four-month-old baby in tow will be reminder enough."

The idea of going into his family's farmhouse and behaving like a nightmare didn't sit as well with her as it had when the plan had been fully abstract. But now he had given names to the family members. Now she had been here for a while. And now it was all starting to feel a little bit real.

"It won't hurt. Though, he's pretty quiet. It might help if he screamed."

She laughed. "Oh, I don't know about that. I have a feeling your mom and sister might just want to hold him. That will be the real problem. Not having everyone hate me. That'll be easy enough. It'll be keeping everyone from loving him."

That comment struck her square in the chest, made her realize just what they were playing at here. She was going to be lying to these people. And yes, the idea was to alienate them, but they were going to think she might be their daughter-in-law, sister-in-law…that Riley would be their grandson or nephew.

But it would be a lie.

That's the point, you moron. And who cares? They're strangers. Riley is your life. He's your responsibility. And you'll never see these people again.

"We won't let them hold the baby," he said, his expression hard, as if he'd suddenly realized she wasn't completely wrong about his mother and sister and it bothered him.

She wished she could understand why he felt so strongly about putting a stop to his father playing matchmaker. As someone whose parents were ambivalent about her existence, his disregard for his family's well wishes was hard to comprehend.

"Okay," she said. "Fine by me. And you just want me to…be my charming self?"

"Obviously we'll have to come up with a story about our relationship. We don't have to make up how we met. We can say we met through the ad."

"The ad your father placed, not the ad you placed."

"Naturally."

She looked at Joshua then, at the broad expanse of table between them. Two people who looked less like a couple probably didn't exist on the face of the planet. Honestly, two strangers standing across the street from each other probably looked more like a happily engaged unit than they did.

She frowned. "This is very unconvincing."

"What is? Be specific."

She rolled her eyes at his impatience. "Us."

She stood up and walked toward him, sitting down in the chair right next to him. She looked at him for a moment, at the sharp curve of his jaw, the enticing shape of his lips. He was an attractive man. That was an understatement. He was also so uptight she was pretty sure he had a stick up his ass.

"Look, you want your family to think you've lost your mind, to think you have hooked up with a totally unsuitable woman, right?"

"That is the game."

"Then you have to look like you've lost your mind over me. Unfortunately, Joshua, you look very much in your right mind. In fact, a man of sounder mind may not exist. You are…responsible. You literally look like The Man."

"Which man?"

"Like, The Man. Like, fight the power. *You're* the power. Nobody's going to believe you're with me. At least, not if you don't seem a little bit… looser."

A slight smile tipped up those lips she had been thinking about only a moment before. His blue eyes warmed, and she felt an answering warmth spread low in her belly. "So what you're saying is we need to look like we have more of a connection?"

Her throat went dry. "It's just a suggestion."

He leaned forward, his gaze intent on hers. "An

essential one, I think." Then he reached up and she jerked backward, nearly toppling off the side of her chair. "It looks like I'm not the only one who's wound a bit tight."

"I'm not," she said, taking a deep breath, trying to get her jittery body to calm itself down.

She wasn't used to men. She wasn't used to men touching her. Yes, intermittently she and her mother had lived with some of her mother's boyfriends, but none of them had ever been inappropriate with her. And she had never been close enough to even give any of them hugs.

And she really, really wasn't used to men who were so beautiful it was almost physically painful to look directly at them.

"You're right. We have to do a better job of looking like a couple. And that would include you not scampering under the furniture when I get close to you."

She sat up straight and folded her hands in her lap. "I did not scamper," she muttered.

"You were perilously close to a scamper."

"Was not," she grumbled, and then her breath caught in her throat as his warm palm made contact with her cheek.

He slid his thumb down the curve of her face to that dent just beneath her lips, his eyes never leaving hers. She felt...stunned and warm. No, hot. So very hot. Like there was a furnace inside that had been turned up the moment his hand touched her bare skin.

She supposed she was meant to be flirtatious. To play the part of the moneygrubbing tart with loose morals he needed her to be, that his family would expect her to be. But right now, she was shocked into immobility.

She took a deep breath, fighting for composure. But his thumb migrated from the somewhat reasonable point just below her mouth to her lip and her composure dissolved completely. His touch felt…shockingly intimate and filthy somehow. Not in a bad way, just in a way she'd never experienced before.

For some reason she would never be able to articulate—not even to herself—she darted her tongue out and touched the tip to his thumb. She tasted salt, skin and a promise that arrowed downward to the most private part of her body, leaving her feeling breathless. Leaving her feeling new somehow.

As if a wholly unexpected and previously unknown part of herself had been uncovered, awoken. She wanted to do exactly what he had accused her of doing earlier. She wanted to turn away. Wanted to scurry beneath the furniture or off into the night. Somewhere safe. Somewhere less confrontational.

But he was still looking at her. And those blue eyes were like chains, lashing her to the seat, holding her in place. And his thumb, pressed against her lip, felt heavy. Much too heavy for her to push against. For her to fight.

And when it came right down to it, she didn't even want to.

Something expanded in her chest, spreading low, opening up a yawning chasm in her stomach. Deepening her need, her want. Her desire for things she hadn't known she could desire until now.

Until he had made a promise with his touch that she hadn't known she wanted fulfilled.

She was just about to come back to herself, to pull away. And then he closed the distance between them.

His lips were warm and firm. The kiss was nothing like she had imagined it might be. She had always thought a kiss must reach inside and steal your brain. Transform you. She had always imagined a kiss to be powerful, considering the way her mother acted.

When her mother was under the influence of love—at least, that was what her mother had called it; Danielle had always known it was lust—she acted like someone entirely apart from herself.

Yes, Danielle had always known a kiss could be powerful. But what she hadn't counted on was that she might feel wholly like *herself* when a man fused his lips to hers. That she would be so perfectly aware of where she was, of what she was doing.

Of the pressure of his lips against hers, the warmth of his hand as he cradled her face, the hard, tightening knot of desire in her stomach that told her how insufficient the kiss was.

The desire that told her just how much more she wanted. Just how much more there could be.

He was kissing her well, this near stranger, and she never wanted it to end.

Instinctively, she angled her head slightly, parting her lips, allowing him to slide his tongue against hers. It was unexpectedly slick, unexpectedly arousing. Unexpectedly everything she wanted.

That was the other thing that surprised her. Because not only had she imagined a woman might lose herself entirely when a man kissed her, she had also imagined she would be immune. Because she knew better. She knew the cost. But she was sitting here, allowing him to kiss her and kiss her and kiss her. She was Danielle Kelly, and she was submitting herself to this sensual assault with almost shocking abandon.

Her hands were still folded in her lap, almost primly, but her mouth was parted wide, gratefully receiving every stroke of his tongue, slow and languorous against her own. Sexy. Deliciously affecting.

He moved his hands then, sliding them around the back of her neck, down between her shoulder blades, along the line of her spine until his hands spanned her waist. She arched, wishing she could press her body against his. Wishing she could do something to close the distance between them. Because he was still sitting in his chair and she in hers.

He pulled away, and she followed him, leaning into him with an almost humiliating desperation, wanting to taste him again. To be kissed again. By Joshua Grayson, the man she was committing an insane kind of fraud with. The man who had hired her to play the part of his pretend fiancée.

"That will do," he said, lifting his hand and squeezing her chin gently, those blue eyes glinting with a sharpness that cut straight to her soul. "Yes, Ms. Kelly, that will do quite nicely."

Then he released his hold on her completely, settling back in his seat, his attention returning to his dinner plate.

A slash of heat bled across Danielle's cheekbones. He hadn't felt anything at all. He had been proving a point. Just practicing the ruse they would be performing for his family tomorrow night. The kiss hadn't changed anything for him at all. Hadn't been more than the simple meeting of mouths.

It had been her first kiss. It had been everything.

And right then she got her first taste of just how badly a man could make a woman feel. Of how—when wounded—feminine pride could be a treacherous and testy thing.

She rose from her seat and rounded to stand behind his. Then, without fully pausing to think about what she might be doing, she placed her hands on his shoulders, leaned forward and slid her hands beneath the collar of his shirt and down his chest.

Her palms made contact with his hot skin, with hard muscle, and she had to bite her lip to keep from groaning out loud. She had to plant her feet firmly on the wood floor to keep herself from running away, from jerking her hands back like a child burned on a hot oven.

She'd never touched a man like this before. It was shocking just how arousing she found it, this little form of revenge, this little rebellion against his blasé response to the earthquake he had caused in her body.

She leaned her head forward, nearly pressing her lips against his ear. Then her teeth scraped his earlobe.

"Yes," she whispered. "I think it's quite convincing."

She straightened again, slowly running her fingernails over his skin as she did. She didn't know where this confidence had come from. Where the know-how and seemingly deep, feminine instinct had come from that allowed her to toy with him. But there it was.

She was officially playing the part of a saucy minx. Considering that was what he had hired her for, her flirtation was a good thing. But her heart thundered harder than a drum as she walked back to Riley, picked up his carrier and flipped her hair as she turned to face Joshua.

"I think I'm going to bed. I had best prepare myself to meet your family."

"You'll be wearing something different tomorrow," he said, his tone firm.

"Why?" She looked down at her ragged sweatshirt and skinny jeans. "That doesn't make any sense. You wanted me to look unsuitable. I might as well go in this."

"No, you brought up a very good point. You have to look unsuitable, but this situation also has to be believable. Plus, I think a gold digger would demand a new wardrobe, don't you?" One corner of his lips quirked upward, and she had a feeling he was punishing her for her little display a moment ago.

If only she could work out quite where the trap was.

"I don't know," she said, her voice stiff.

"But, Ms. Kelly, you told me yourself that you

are a gold digger. That's why you're here, after all. For my gold."

"I suppose so," she said, keeping her words deliberately hard. "But I want actual gold, not clothes. So this is another thing that's going to be on you."

Those blue eyes glinted, and right then she got an idea of just how dangerous he was to her. "Consider it done."

And if there was one thing she had learned so far about Joshua Grayson, it was that if he said something would be done, it would be.

Five

Joshua wasn't going to try to turn Danielle into a sophisticate overnight. He was also avoiding thinking about the way it had felt to kiss her soft lips. Was avoiding remembering the way her hands had felt sliding down his chest.

He needed to make sure the two of them looked like a couple, that much was true. But he wouldn't allow himself to be distracted by her. There were a million reasons not to touch Danielle Kelly—unless they were playing a couple. Yes, there would have to be some touching, but he was not going to take advantage of her.

First of all, she was at his financial mercy. Second of all, she was the kind of woman who came with entanglements. And he didn't want any entanglements.

He wasn't the type to have trouble with self-control. If it wasn't a good time to seek out a physical relationship, he didn't. It wasn't a good time now, which meant he would defer any kind of sexual gratification until the end of his association with Danielle.

That should be fine.

He should be able to consider any number of women who he had on-again, off-again associations with, choose one and get in touch with her after Danielle left. His mind and body should be set on that.

Sadly, all he could think of was last night's kiss and the shocking heat that had come with it.

And then Danielle came down the stairs wearing the simple black dress he'd had delivered for her.

His thoughts about not transforming her into a sophisticated woman overnight held true. Her long, straight brown hair still hung limp down to her waist, and she had no makeup on to speak of except pale pink gloss on her lips.

But the simple cut of the dress suited her slender figure and displayed small, perky breasts that had been hidden beneath her baggy, threadbare sweaters.

She was holding on to the handle of the baby's car seat with both hands, lugging it down the stairs. For one moment, he was afraid she might topple over. He moved forward quickly, grabbing the handle and taking the seat from her.

When he looked down at the sleeping child, a strange tightness invaded his chest. "It wouldn't be good for you or for Riley if you fell and broke your neck trying to carry something that's too heavy for you," he said, his tone harder than he'd intended it to be.

Danielle scowled. "Well, offer assistance earlier next time. I had to get down the stairs somehow. Anyway, I've been navigating stairs like this with the baby since he was born. I lived in an apartment. On the third floor."

"I imagine he's heavier now than he used to be."

"An expert on child development?" She arched one dark brow as she posed the question.

He gritted his teeth. "Hardly."

She stepped away from the stairs, and the two of them walked toward the door. Just because he wanted to make it clear that he was in charge of the evening, he placed his hand low on her back, right at the dip where her spine curved, right above what the dress revealed to be a magnificent ass.

He had touched her there to get to her, but he had not anticipated the touch getting to him.

He ushered her out quickly, then handed the car

seat to her, allowing her to snap it into the base—the one he'd had installed in his car when all of the nursery accoutrements had been delivered—then sat waiting for her to get in.

As they started to pull out of the driveway, she wrapped her arms around herself, rubbing her hands over her bare skin. "Do you think you could turn the heater on?"

He frowned. "Why didn't you bring a jacket?"

"I don't have one? All I have are my sweaters. And I don't think either of them would go with the dress. Would kind of ruin the effect."

He put the brakes on, slipped out of his own jacket and handed it to her. She just looked at him like he was offering her a live gopher. "Take it," he said.

She frowned but reached out, taking the jacket and slipping it on. "Thank you," she said, her voice sounding hollow.

They drove to his parents' house in silence, the only sounds coming from the baby sitting in the back seat. A sobering reminder of the evening that was about to unfold. He was going to present a surprise fiancée and a surprise baby to his parents, and suddenly, he didn't look at this plan in quite the same way as he had before.

He was throwing Danielle into the deep end. Throwing Riley into the deep end.

Joshua gritted his teeth, tightening his hold on

the steering wheel. Finally, the interminable drive through town was over. He turned left off a winding road and onto a dirt drive that led back to the familiar, humble farmhouse his parents still called home.

That some part of his heart still called home too.

He looked over at Danielle, who had gone pale. "It's fine," he said.

Danielle looked down at the ring on her finger, then back up at him. "I guess it's showtime."

Danielle felt warm all over, no longer in need of Joshua's jacket, and conflicted down to the brand-new shoes Joshua had ordered for her.

But it wasn't the dress, or the shoes, that had her feeling warm. It was the jacket. Well, obviously a jacket was supposed to make her warm, but this was different. Joshua had realized she was cold. And it had mattered to him.

He had given her his own jacket so she could keep warm.

It was too big, the sleeves went well past the edges of her fingertips, and it smelled like him. From the moment she had slipped it on, she had been fighting the urge to bury her nose in the fabric and lose herself in the sharp, masculine smell that reminded her of his skin. Skin she had tasted last night.

Standing on the front step of this modest farmhouse that she could hardly believe Joshua had ever lived in, wearing his coat, with him holding Riley's car seat, it was too easy to believe this actually was some kind of "meet the parents" date.

In effect, she supposed it was. She was even wearing his jacket. His jacket that was still warm from his body and smelled—

Danielle was still ruminating about the scent of Joshua's jacket when the door opened. A blonde woman with graying hair and blue eyes that looked remarkably like her son's gave them a warm smile.

"Joshua," she said, glancing sideways at Danielle and clearly doing her best not to look completely shocked, "I didn't expect you so early. And I didn't know you were bringing a guest." Her eyes fell to the carrier in Joshua's hand. "Two guests."

"I thought it would be a good surprise."

"What would be?"

A man who could only be Joshua's father came to the door behind the woman. He was tall, with dark hair and eyes. He looked nice too. They both did. There was a warmth to them, a kindness, that didn't seem to be present in their son.

But then Danielle felt the warmth of the jacket again, and she had to revise that thought. Joshua might not exude kindness, but it was definitely there, buried. And for the life of her, she couldn't figure out why he hid it.

She was prickly and difficult, but at least she

had an excuse. Her family was the worst. As far as she could tell, his family was guilty of caring too much. And she just couldn't feel that sorry for a rich dude whose parents loved him and were involved in his life more than he wanted them to be.

"Who is this?" Joshua's father asked.

"Danielle, this is my mom and dad, Todd and Nancy Grayson. Mom, Dad, this is Danielle Kelly," Joshua said smoothly. "And I have you to thank for meeting her, Dad."

His father's eyebrows shot upward. "Do you?"

"Yes," Joshua said. "She responded to your ad. Mom, Dad, Danielle is my fiancée."

They were ushered into the house quickly after that announcement, and there were a lot of exclamations. The house was already full. A young woman sat in the corner holding hands with a large, tattooed man who was built like a brick house and was clearly related to Joshua somehow. There was another man, as tall as Joshua, with slightly darker hair and the same blue eyes but who didn't carry himself quite as stiffly. His build was somewhere in between Joshua and the tattooed man, muscular but not a beast.

"My brother Devlin," Joshua said, indicating the tattooed man before putting his arm around Danielle's waist as they moved deeper into the room, "and his wife, Mia. And this is my brother

Isaiah. I'm surprised his capable assistant, Poppy, isn't somewhere nearby."

"Isaiah, did you want a beer or whiskey?" A petite woman appeared from the kitchen area, her curly, dark hair swept back into a bun, a few stray pieces bouncing around her pretty face. She was impeccable. From that elegant updo down to the soles of her tiny, high-heeled feet. She was wearing a high-waisted skirt that flared out at the hips and fell down past her knees, along with a plain, fitted top.

"Is that his…girlfriend?" Danielle asked.

Poppy laughed. "Absolutely not," she said, her tone clipped. "I'm his assistant."

Danielle thought it strange that an assistant would be at a family gathering but didn't say anything.

"She's more than an assistant," Nancy Grayson said. "She's part of the family. She's been with them since they started the business."

Danielle had not been filled in on the details of his family's relationships because she only needed to know how to alienate them, not how to endear herself to them.

The front door opened again and this time it was a younger blonde woman whose eyes also matched Joshua's who walked in. "Sorry I'm late," she said, "I got caught up working on a project."

This had to be his sister, Faith. The architect

he talked about with such pride and fondness. A woman who was Danielle's age and yet so much more successful they might be completely different species.

"This is Joshua's fiancée," Todd Grayson said. "He's engaged."

"Shut the front door," Faith said. "Are you really?"

"Yes," Joshua said, the lie rolling easily off his tongue.

Danielle bit back a comment about his PR skills. She was supposed to be hard to deal with, but they weren't supposed to call attention to the fact this was a ruse.

"That's great?" Faith took a step forward and hugged her brother, then leaned in to grab hold of Danielle, as well.

"Is nobody going to ask about the baby?" Isaiah asked.

"Obviously *you* are," Devlin said.

"Well, it's kind of the eight-hundred-pound gorilla in the room. Or the ten-pound infant."

"It's my baby," Danielle said, feeling color mount in her cheeks.

She noticed a slight shift in Joshua's father's expression. Which was the general idea. To make him suspicious of her. To make him think he had gone and caught his son a gold digger.

"Well, that's…" She could see Joshua's mother

searching for words. "It's definitely unexpected." She looked apologetically at Danielle the moment the words left her mouth. "It's just that Joshua hasn't shown much interest in marriage or family."

Danielle had a feeling that was an understatement. If Joshua was willing to go to such lengths to get his father out of his business, then he must be about as anti-marriage as you could get.

"Well," Joshua said, "Danielle and I met because of Dad."

His mother's blue gaze sharpened. "How?"

His father looked guilty. "Well, I thought he could use a little help," he said finally.

"What kind of help?"

"It's not good for a man to be alone, especially not our boys," he said insistently.

"Some of us like to be alone," Isaiah pointed out.

"You wouldn't feel that way if you didn't have a woman who cooked for you and ran your errands," his father responded, looking pointedly at Poppy.

"She's an employee," Isaiah said.

Poppy looked more irritated and distressed by Isaiah's comment than she did by the Grayson family patriarch's statement. But she didn't say anything.

"You were right," Joshua said. "I just needed to find the right woman. You placed that ad, listing all of my assets, and the right woman responded."

This was so ridiculous. Danielle felt her face heating. The assets Joshua's father had listed were his bank account, and there was no way in the world that wasn't exactly what everyone in his family was thinking.

She knew this was her chance to confirm her gold-digging motives. But right then, Riley started to cry.

"Oh," she said, feeling flustered. "Just let me… I need to…".

She fumbled around with the new diaper bag, digging around for a bottle, and then went over to the car seat, taking the baby out of it.

"Let me help," Joshua's mother said.

She was being so kind. Danielle felt terrible.

But before Danielle could protest, the other woman was taking Riley from her arms. Riley wiggled and fussed, but then she efficiently plucked the bottle from Danielle's hand and stuck it right in his mouth. He quieted immediately.

"What a good baby," she said. "Does he usually go to strangers?"

Danielle honestly didn't know. "Other than a neighbor whose known him since he was born, I'm the only one who takes care of him," she said.

"Don't you have any family?"

Danielle shook her head, feeling every inch the curiosity she undoubtedly was. Every single eye in the room was trained on her, and she knew they were all waiting for her to make a mistake. She was *supposed* to make a mistake, dammit. That was what Joshua was paying her to do.

"I don't have any family," she said decisively. "It's just been me and Riley from the beginning."

"It must be nice to have some help now," Faith said, not unkindly, but definitely probing.

"It is," Danielle said. "I mean, it's really hard taking care of a baby by yourself. And I didn't make enough money to…well, anything. So meeting Joshua has been great. Because he's so…helpful."

A timer went off in the other room and Joshua's mother blinked. "Oh, I have to get dinner." She turned to her son. "Since you're so helpful, Joshua." And before Danielle could protest, before Joshua could protest, Nancy dumped Riley right into his arms.

He looked like he'd been handed a bomb. And frankly, Danielle felt a little bit like a bomb might detonate at any moment. It had not escaped her notice that Joshua had never touched Riley. Yes, he had carried his car seat, but he had never voluntarily touched the baby. Which, now that she thought about it, must have been purposeful. But then, not everybody liked babies. She had never been particularly drawn to them before Riley. Maybe Joshua felt the same way.

She could tell by his awkward posture, and the way Riley's small frame was engulfed by Joshua's large, muscular one, that any contact with babies was not something he was used to.

She imagined Joshua's reaction would go a long way in proving how unsuitable she was. Maybe not in the way he had hoped, but it definitely made his point.

He took a seat on the couch, still holding on to Riley, still clearly committed to the farce.

"So you met through an ad," Isaiah said, his voice full of disbelief. "An ad that Dad put in the paper."

Everyone's head swiveled, and they looked at Todd. "I did what any concerned father would do for his son."

Devlin snorted. "Thank God I found a wife on my own."

"You found a wife by pilfering from my friendship pool," Faith said, her tone disapproving. "Isaiah and Joshua have too much class to go picking out women that young."

"Actually," Danielle said, deciding this was the perfect opportunity to highlight another of the many ways in which she was unsuitable, "I'm only twenty-two."

Joshua's father looked at him, his gaze sharp. "Really?"

"Really," Danielle said.

"That's unexpected," Todd said to his son.

"That's what's so great about how we met,"

Joshua said. "Had I looked for a life partner on my own, I probably would have chosen somebody with a completely different set of circumstances. Had you asked me only a few short weeks ago, I would have said I didn't want children. And now look at me."

Everybody *was* looking at him, and it was clear he was extremely uncomfortable. Danielle wasn't entirely sure he was making the point he hoped to make, but he did make a pretty amusing picture. "I also would have chosen somebody closer to my age. But the great thing about Danielle is that she is so mature. I think it's because she's a mother. And yes, it happened for her in non-ideal circumstances, but her ability to rise above her situation and solve her problems—namely by responding to the ad—is one of the many things I find attractive about her."

She wanted to kick him in the shin. He was being an asshole, and he was making her sound like a total flake... But that was the whole idea. And, honestly, given the information Joshua had about her life...he undoubtedly thought she *was* a flake. It was stupid, and it wasn't fair. One of the many things she had learned about people since becoming the sole caregiver for Riley was that even though everyone had sex, a woman was an immediate pariah the minute she bore the evidence of that sex.

All that mattered to the hypocrites was that Danielle appeared to be a scarlet woman, therefore she was one.

Never mind that in reality she was a virgin.

Which was not a word she needed to be thinking while sitting in the Grayson family living room.

Her cheeks felt hot, like they were being stung by bees.

"Fate is a funny thing," Danielle said, edging closer to Joshua. She took Riley out of his arms, and from the way Joshua surrendered the baby, she could tell he was more than ready to hand him over.

The rest of the evening passed in a blur of awkward moments and stilted conversation. It was clear to her that his family was wonderful and warm, but that they were also seriously questioning Joshua's decision making. Todd Grayson looked as if he was going to be physically assaulted by his wife.

Basically, everything was going according to Joshua's plan.

But Danielle couldn't feel happy about it. She couldn't feel triumphant. It just felt awful.

Finally, it was time to go, and Danielle was ready to scurry out the door and keep on scurrying away from the entire Grayson family—Joshua included.

She was gathering her things, and Joshua was talking to one of his brothers, when Faith approached.

"We haven't gotten a chance to talk yet," she said.

"I guess not," Danielle said, feeling instantly wary. She had a feeling that being approached by Joshua's younger sister like this wouldn't end well.

"I'm sure he's told you all about me," Faith said, and Danielle had a feeling that statement was a test.

"Of course he has." She sounded defensive, even though there was no reason for her to feel defensive, except that she kind of did anyway.

"Great. So here's the thing. I don't know exactly what's going on here, but my brother is not a 'marriage and babies' kind of guy. My brother dates a seemingly endless stream of models, all of whom are about half a foot taller than you without their ridiculous high heels on. Also, he likes blondes."

Danielle felt her face heating again as the other woman appraised her and found her lacking. "Right. Well. Maybe I'm a really great conversationalist. Although, it could be the fact that I don't have a gag reflex."

She watched the other woman's cheeks turn bright pink and felt somewhat satisfied. Unsophisticated, virginal Danielle had made the clearly much more sophisticated Faith Grayson blush.

"Right. Well, if you're leading him around by his…*you know*…so you can get into his wallet, I'm not going to allow that. There's a reason he's avoided commitment all this time. And I'm not going to let you hurt him. He's been hurt enough," she said.

Danielle could only wonder what that meant, because Joshua seemed bulletproof.

"I'm not going to break up with him," Danielle said. "Why would I do that? I'd rather stay in his house than in a homeless shelter."

She wanted to punch her own face. And she was warring with the fact that Faith had rightly guessed that she was using Joshua for his money— though not in the way his sister assumed. And Danielle needed Faith to think the worst. But it also hurt to have her assume something so negative based on Danielle's circumstances. Based on her appearance.

People had been looking at Danielle and judging her as low-class white trash for so long—not exactly incorrectly—that it was a sore spot.

"We're a close family," Faith said. "And we look out for each other. Just remember that."

"Well, your brother loves me."

"If that's true," Faith said, "then I hope you're very happy together. I actually do hope it's true. But the problem is, I'm not sure I believe it."

"Why?" Danielle was bristling, and there

was no reason on earth why she should be. She shouldn't be upset about this. She shouldn't be taking it personally. But she was.

Faith Grayson had taken one look at Danielle and judged her. Pegged her for exactly the kind of person she was, really—a low-class nobody who needed the kind of money and security a man like Joshua could provide. Danielle had burned her pride to the ground to take part in this charade. Poking at the embers of that pride was stupid. But she felt compelled to do it anyway.

"Is it because I'm some kind of skank he would never normally sully himself with?"

"Mostly, it's because I know my brother. And I know he never intended to be in any kind of serious relationship again."

Again.

That word rattled around inside of Danielle. It implied he had been in a serious relationship before. He hadn't mentioned that. He'd just said he didn't want his father meddling. Didn't want marriage. He hadn't said it was because he'd tried before.

She blinked.

Faith took that momentary hesitation and ran with it. "So you don't know that much about him. You don't actually know anything about him, do you? You just know he's rich."

"And he's hot," Danielle said.

She wasn't going to back down. Not now. But she would have a few very grumpy words with Joshua once they left.

He hadn't prepared her for this. She looked like an idiot. As she gathered her things, she realized looking like an idiot was his objective. She could look bad in a great many ways, after all. The fact that they might be an unsuitable couple because she didn't know anything about him would be one way to accomplish that.

When she and Joshua finally stepped outside, heading back to the car amid a thunderous farewell from the family, Danielle felt like she could breathe for the first time in at least two hours. She hadn't realized it, but being inside that house—all warm and cozy and filled with the kind of love she had only ever seen in movies—had made her throat and lungs and chest, and even her fingers, feel tight.

They got into the car, and Danielle folded her arms tightly, leaning her head against the cold passenger-side window, her breath fanning out across the glass, leaving mist behind. She didn't bother fighting the urge to trace a heart in it.

"Feeling that in character?" Joshua asked, his tone dry, as he put the car in Reverse and began to pull out of the driveway.

She stuck her tongue out and scribbled over the heart. "Not particularly. I don't understand. Now that I've met them, I understand even less. Your sister grilled me the minute she got a chance to talk to me alone. Your father is worried about the situation. Your mother is trying to be supportive in spite of the fact that we are clearly the worst couple of all time. And you're doing this why, Joshua? I don't understand."

She hadn't meant to call him out in quite that way. After all, what did she care about his motivations? He was paying her. The fact that he was a rich, eccentric idiot kind of worked in her favor. But tonight had felt wrong. And while she was more into survival than into the nuances of right and wrong, the ruse was getting to her.

"I explained to you already," he said, his tone so hard it elicited a small, plaintive cry from Riley in the back.

"Don't wake up the baby," she snapped.

"We really are a convincing couple," he responded.

"Not to your sister. Who told me we didn't make any sense together because you had never shown any interest in falling in love *again*."

It was dark in the car, so she felt rather than saw the tension creep up his spine. It was in the way he shifted in his seat, how his fists rolled forward as he twisted his hands on the steering wheel.

"Well," he said, "that's the thing. They all know. Because family like mine doesn't leave well enough alone. They want to know about all your injuries, all your scars, and then they obsess over the idea that they might be able to heal them. And they don't listen when you tell them healing is not necessary."

"Right," she said, blowing out an exasperated breath. "Here's the thing. I'm just a dumb bimbo you picked up through a newspaper ad who needed your money. So I don't understand all this coded nonsense. Just tell me what's going on. Especially if I'm going to spend more nights trying to alienate your family—who are basically a childhood sitcom fantasy of what a family should be."

"I've done it before, Danielle. Love. It's not worth it. Not considering how badly it hurts when it ends. But even more, it's not worth it when you consider how badly you can hurt the other person."

His words fell flat in the car, and she didn't know how to respond to them. "I don't…"

"Details aren't important. You've been hurt before, haven't you?"

He turned the car off the main road and headed up the long drive to his house. She took a deep breath. "Yes."

"By Riley's father?"

She shifted uncomfortably. "Not exactly."

"You didn't love him?"

"No," she said. "I didn't love him. But my mother kind of did a number on me. I do understand that love hurts. I also understand that a supportive family is not necessarily guaranteed."

"Yeah," Joshua said, "supportive family is great." He put the car in Park and killed the engine before getting out and stalking toward the house.

Danielle frowned, then unbuckled quickly, getting out of the car and pushing the sleeves of Joshua's jacket back so she could get Riley's car seat out of the base. Then she headed up the stairs and into the house after him.

"And yet you are trying to hurt yours. So excuse me if I'm not making all the connections."

"I'm not trying to hurt my family," he said, turning around, pushing his hand through his blond hair. His blue eyes glittered, his jaw suddenly looking sharper, his cheekbones more hollow. "What I want is for them to leave well enough alone. My father doesn't understand. He thinks all I need is to find somebody to love again and I'm going to be fixed. But there is no fixing this. There's no fixing me. I don't want it. And yeah, maybe this scheme is over the top, but don't you think putting an ad in the paper looking for a wife for your son is over the top too? I'm not giving him back anything he didn't dish out."

"Maybe you could talk to him."

"You think I haven't talked to him? You think this was my first resort? You're wrong about that.

I tried reasonable discourse, but you can't reason with an unreasonable man."

"Yeah," Danielle said, picking at the edge of her thumbnail. "He seemed like a real monster. What with the clear devotion to your mother, the fact that he raised all of you, that he supported you well enough that you could live in that house all your life and then go off to become more successful than he was."

She set the car seat down on the couch and unbuckled it, lifting Riley into her arms and heading toward the stairs.

"We didn't have anything when I was growing up," he said, his tone flat and strange.

Danielle swallowed hard, lifting her hand to cradle Riley's soft head. "I'm sorry. But unless you were homeless or were left alone while one of your parents went to work all day—and I mean *alone*, not with siblings—then we might have different definitions of nothing."

"Fine," he said. "We weren't that poor. But we didn't have anything extra, and there was definitely nothing to do around here but get into trouble when you didn't have money."

She blinked. "What kind of trouble?"

"The usual kind. Go out to the woods, get messed up, have sex."

"Last I checked, condoms and drugs cost

money." She held on to Riley a little bit tighter. "Pretty sure you could have bought a movie ticket."

He lifted his shoulder. "Look, we pooled our money. We did what we did. Didn't worry about the future, didn't worry about anything."

"What changed?" Because obviously something had. He hadn't stayed here. He hadn't stayed aimless.

"One day I looked up and realized this was all I would ever have unless I changed something. Let me tell you, that's pretty sobering. A future of farming, barely making it, barely scraping by? That's what my dad had. And I hated it. I drank in the woods every night with my friends to avoid that reality. I didn't want to have my dad's life. So I made some changes. Not really soon enough to improve my grades or get myself a full scholarship, but I ended up moving to Seattle and getting myself an entry-level job with a PR firm."

"You just moved? You didn't know anybody?"

"No. I didn't know anyone. But I met people. And, it turned out, I was good at meeting people. Which was interesting because you don't meet very many new people in a small town that you've lived in your entire life. But in Seattle, no one knew me. No one knew who my father was, and no one had expectations for me. I was judged entirely on my own merit, and I could completely rewrite who I was. Not just some small-town deadbeat, but a young, bright kid who had a future in front of him."

The way he told that story, the very idea of it, was tantalizing to Danielle. The idea of starting over. Having a clean slate. Of course, with a baby in tow, a change like that would be much more difficult. But her association with Joshua would allow her to make it happen.

It was…shocking to realize he'd had to start over once. Incredibly encouraging, even though she was feeling annoyed with him at the moment.

She leaned forward and absently pressed a kiss to Riley's head. "That must've been incredible. And scary."

"The only scary thing was the idea of going back to where I came from without changing anything. So I didn't allow that to happen. I worked harder than everybody else. I set goals and I met them. And then I met Shannon."

Something ugly twisted inside of Danielle's stomach the moment he said the other woman's name. For the life of her she couldn't figure out why. She felt…curious. But in a desperate way. Like she needed to know everything about this other person. This person who had once shared Joshua's life. This person who had undoubtedly made him the man standing in front of her. If she didn't know about this woman, then she would never understand him.

"What, then? Who was Shannon?" Her desperation was evident in her words, and she didn't bother hiding it.

"She was my girlfriend. For four years, while I was getting established in Seattle. We lived together. I was going to ask her to marry me."

He looked away from her then, something in his blue eyes turning distant. "Then she found out she was pregnant, and I figured I could skip the elaborate proposal and move straight to the wedding."

She knew him well enough to know this story wasn't headed toward a happy ending. He didn't have a wife. He didn't have a child. In fact, she was willing to bet he'd never had a child. Based on the way he interacted with Riley. Or rather, the very practiced way he avoided interacting with Riley.

"That didn't happen," she said, because she didn't know what else to say, and part of her wanted to spare him having to tell the rest of the story. But, also, part of her needed to know.

"She wanted to plan the wedding. She wanted to wait until after the baby was born. You know, wedding dress sizes and stuff like that. So I agreed. She miscarried late, Danielle. Almost five months. It was…the most physically harrowing thing I've ever watched anyone go through. But the recovery was worse. And I didn't know what to do. So I went back to work. We had a nice apartment, we had a view of the city, and if I worked, she didn't have to. I could support her, I could buy her things. I could do my best to make her happy, keep her focused on the wedding."

He had moved so quickly through the devastating, painful revelation of his lost baby that she barely had time to process it. But she also realized he had to tell the story this way. There was no point lingering on the details. It was simple fact. He had been with a woman he loved very much. He had intended to marry her, had been expecting a child with her. And they had lost the baby.

She held on a little bit more tightly to Riley.

"She kept getting worse. Emotionally. She moved into a different bedroom, then she didn't get out of bed. She had a lot of pain. At first, I didn't question it, because it seemed reasonable that she'd need pain medication after what she went through. But then she kept taking it. And I wondered if that was okay. We had a fight about it. She said it wasn't right for me to question her pain—physical or otherwise—when all I did was work. And you know…I thought she was probably right. So I let it go. For a year, I let it go. And then I found out the situation with the prescription drugs was worse than I realized. But when I confronted Shannon, she just got angry."

It was so strange for Danielle to imagine what he was telling her. This whole other life he'd had. In a city where he had lived with a woman and loved her. Where he had dreamed of having a family. Of having a child. Where he had buried himself in work to avoid dealing with the pain of loss, while the woman he loved lost herself in a different way.

The tale seemed so far removed from the man he was now. From this place, from that hard set to his jaw, that sharp glitter in his eye, the way he held his shoulders straight. She couldn't imagine this man feeling at a loss. Feeling helpless.

"She got involved with another man, someone I worked with. Maybe it started before she left me, but I'm not entirely sure. All I know is she wasn't sleeping with me at the time, so even if she was with him before she moved out, it hardly felt like cheating. And anyway, the affair wasn't really the important part. That guy was into recreational drug use. It's how he functioned. And he made it all available to her."

"That's…that's awful, Joshua. I know how bad that stuff can be. I've seen it."

He shook his head. "Do you have any idea what it's like? To have somebody come into your life who's beautiful, happy, and to watch her leave your life as something else entirely. Broken, an addict. I ruined her."

Danielle took a step back, feeling as though she had been struck by the impact of his words. "No, you didn't. It was drugs. It was…"

"I wasn't there for her. I didn't know how to be. I didn't like hard things, Danielle. I never did. I didn't want to stay in Copper Ridge and work the land—I didn't want to deal with a lifetime of scraping by, because it was too hard."

"Right. You're so lazy that you moved to Seattle and started from scratch and worked your way to the highest ranks of the company? I don't buy that."

"There's reward in that kind of work, though. And you don't have to deal with your life when it gets bad. You just go work more. And you can tell yourself it's fine because you're making more money. Because you're making your life easier, life for the other person easier, even while you let them sit on the couch slowly dying, waiting for you to help them. I convinced myself that what I was doing was important. It was the worst kind of narcissism, Danielle, and I'm not going to excuse it."

"But that was… It was a unique circumstance. And you're different. And…it's not like every future relationship…"

"And here's the problem. You don't know me. You don't even like me and yet you're trying to fix this. You're trying to convince me I should give relationships another try. It's your first instinct, and you don't even actually care. My father can't stop any more than you could stop yourself just now. So I did this." He gestured between the two of them. "I did this because he escalated it all the way to putting an ad in the paper. Because he won't listen to me. Because he knows my ex is a junkie somewhere living on the damned street, and that I feel responsible for that, and still he wants me to live his life. This life here, where he's never made a single mistake or let anyone down."

Danielle had no idea what to say to that. She imagined that his dad had made mistakes. But what did she know? She only knew about absentee fathers and mothers who treated their children like afterthoughts.

Her arms were starting to ache. Her chest ached too. All of her ached.

"I'm going to take Riley up to bed," she said, turning and heading up the stairs.

She didn't look back, but she could hear the heavy footfalls behind her, and she knew he was following her. Even if she didn't quite understand why.

She walked into her bedroom, and she left the door open. She crossed the space and set Riley down in the crib. He shifted for a moment, stretching his arms up above his head and kicking his feet out. But he didn't wake up. She was sweaty from having his warm little body pressed against her chest, but she was grateful for that feeling now. Thinking about Joshua and his loss made her feel especially grateful.

Joshua was standing in the doorway, looking at her. "Did you still want to argue with me?"

She shook her head. "I never wanted to argue with you."

She went to walk past him, but his big body blocked her path. She took a step toward him, and he refused to move, his blue eyes looking straight into hers.

"You seemed like you wanted to argue," he responded.

"No," she said, reaching up to press her hand against him, to push him out of the way. "I just wanted an explanation."

The moment her hand made contact with his shoulder, something raced through her. Something electric. Thrilling. Something that reached back to that feeling, that tightening low in her stomach when he'd first mentioned Shannon.

The two feelings were connected.

Jealousy. That was what she felt. Attraction. That was what this was.

She looked up, his chin in her line of sight. She saw a dusting of golden whiskers, and they looked prickly. His chin looked strong. The two things in combination—the strength and the prickliness—made her want to reach out and touch him, to test both of those hypotheses and see if either was true.

Touching him was craziness. She knew it was.

So she curled her fingers into a fist and lowered her hand back down to her side.

"Tell me," he said, his voice rough. "After going through what you did, being pregnant. Being abandoned… You don't want to jump right back into relationships, do you?"

He didn't know the situation. And he didn't know it because she had purposefully kept it from him. Still, because of the circumstances surrounding Riley's birth, because of the way her mother had always conducted relationships with men, because of the way they had always ended, Danielle wanted to avoid romantic entanglements.

So she could find an honest answer in there somewhere.

"I don't want to jump into anything," she said, keeping her voice even. "But there's a difference between being cautious and saying never."

"Is there?"

He had dipped his head slightly, and he seemed to loom over her, to fill her vision, to fill her senses. When she breathed in, the air was scented with him. When she felt warm, the warmth was from his body.

Her lips suddenly felt dry, and she licked them. Then became more aware of them than she'd ever been in her entire life. They felt…obvious. Needy.

She was afraid she knew exactly what they were needy for.

His mouth. His kiss.

The taste of him. The feel of him.

She wondered if he was thinking of their kiss too. Of course, for him, a kiss was probably a commonplace event.

For her, it had been singular.

"You can't honestly say you want to spend the rest of your life alone?"

"I'm only alone when I want to be," he said, his voice husky. "There's a big difference between wanting to share your life with somebody and wanting to share your bed sometimes." He tilted his head to the side. "Tell me. Have you shared your bed with anyone since you were with him?"

She shook her head, words, explanations, getting stuck in her throat. But before she knew it, she couldn't speak anyway, because he had closed the distance between them and claimed her mouth with his.

Six

He was hell bound, that much was certain. After everything that had happened tonight with his family, after Shannon, his fate had been set in stone. But if it hadn't been, then this kiss would have sealed that fate, padlocked it and flung it right down into the fire.

Danielle was young, she was vulnerable and contractually she was at his mercy to a certain degree. Kissing her, wanting to do more with her, was taking being an asshole to extremes.

Right now, he didn't care.

If this was hell, he was happy to hang out for

a while. If only he could keep kissing her, if only he could keep tasting her.

She held still against his body for a moment before angling her head, wrapping her arms around his neck, sliding her fingers through his hair and cupping the back of his head as if she was intent on holding him against her mouth.

As if she was concerned he might break the kiss. As if he was capable of that.

Sanity and reasonable decision making had exited the building the moment he had closed the distance between them. It wasn't coming back anytime soon. Not as long as she continued to make those sweet, kittenish noises. Not as long as she continued to stroke her tongue against his—tentatively at first and then with much more boldness.

He gripped the edge of the doorjamb, backing her against the frame, pressing his body against hers. He was hard, and he knew she would feel just how much he wanted her.

He slipped his hands around her waist, then down her ass to the hem of her dress. He shoved it upward, completely void of any sort of finesse. Void of anything beyond the need and desperation screaming inside of him to be inside her. To be buried so deep he wouldn't remember anything.

Not why he knew her. Why she was here. Not what had happened at his parents' house tonight. Not the horrific, unending sadness that had happened in his beautiful high-rise apartment overlooking the city he'd thought of as his. The penthouse that should have kept him above the struggle and insulated him from hardship.

Yeah, he didn't want to think about any of it.

He didn't want to think of anything but the way Danielle tasted. How soft her skin was to the touch.

Why the hell some skinny, bedraggled urchin had suddenly managed to light a fire inside of him was beyond him.

He didn't really care about the rationale right now. No. He just wanted to be burned.

He moved his hands around, then dipped one between her legs, rubbing his thumb against the silken fabric of her panties. She gasped, arching against him, wrenching her mouth away from his and letting her head fall back against the door frame.

That was an invitation to go further. He shifted his stance, drawing his hand upward and then down beneath the waistband of her underwear. He made contact with slick, damp skin that spoke of her desire for him. He had to clench his teeth to keep from embarrassing himself then and there.

He couldn't remember the last time a woman had affected him like this, if ever. When a simple touch, the promise of release, had pushed him so close to the edge.

When so little had felt like so much.

He stroked her, centering his attention on her clit. Her eyes flew open wide as if he had discovered something completely new. As if she was discovering something completely new. And that did things to him. Things it shouldn't do. Mattered in ways it shouldn't.

Because this shouldn't matter and neither should she.

He pressed his thumb against her chin, leaned forward and captured her open mouth with his.

"I have to have you," he said, the words rough, unpracticed, definitely not the way he usually propositioned a woman.

His words seemed to shock her. Like she had made contact with a naked wire. She went stiff in his arms, and then she pulled away, her eyes wide. "What are we doing?"

She was being utterly sincere, the words unsteady, her expression one of complete surprise and even...fear.

"I'm pretty sure we were about to make love," he said, using a more gentle terminology than he normally would have because of that strange vulnerability lurking in her eyes.

She shook her head, wiggling out of his hold and moving away from the door, backing toward the crib. "We can't do that. We can't." She pressed her hand against her cheek, and she looked so

"4 for 4" MINI-SURVEY

We are prepared to **REWARD** you with 2 FREE books and 2 FREE gifts for completing our MINI SURVEY!

FREE
Value Over
$20!

You'll get...
TWO FREE BOOKS &
TWO FREE GIFTS

just for participating in our Mini Survey!

Dear Reader,

IT'S A FACT: if you answer 4 quick questions, we'll send you 4 FREE REWARDS!

I'm not kidding you. As a leading publisher of women's fiction, we value your opinions... and your time. That's why we are prepared to **reward** you handsomely for completing our mini-survey. In fact, we have 4 Free Rewards for you, including 2 free books and 2 free gifts.

As you may have guessed, that's why our mini-survey is called **"4 for 4".** Answer 4 questions and get 4 Free Rewards. It's that simple!

Thank you for participating in our survey,

Pam Powers

To get your 4 FREE REWARDS:
Complete the survey below and return the insert today to receive 2 FREE BOOKS and 2 FREE GIFTS guaranteed!

"4 for 4" MINI-SURVEY

1 Is reading one of your favorite hobbies?
☐ YES ☐ NO

2 Do you prefer to read instead of watch TV?
☐ YES ☐ NO

3 Do you read newspapers and magazines?
☐ YES ☐ NO

4 Do you enjoy trying new book series with FREE BOOKS?
☐ YES ☐ NO

YES! I have completed the above Mini-Survey. Please send me my 4 FREE REWARDS (worth over $20 retail). I understand that I am under no obligation to buy anything, as explained on the back of this card.

225/326 HDL GMYG

FIRST NAME	LAST NAME

ADDRESS

APT.#	CITY

STATE/PROV.   ZIP/POSTAL CODE

much like a stereotypical distressed female from some 1950s comic that he would have laughed if she hadn't successfully made him feel like he would be the villain in that piece. "It would be… It would be wrong."

"Why exactly?"

"Because. You're paying me to be here. You're paying me to play the part of your fiancée, and if things get physical between us, then I don't understand exactly what separates me from a prostitute."

"I'm not paying you for sex," he said. "I'm paying you to pretend to be my fiancée. I want you. And that's entirely separate from what we're doing here."

She shook her head, her eyes glistening. "Not to me. I already feel horrible. Like the worst person ever, after what I did to your family. After the way we tricked them tonight. After the way we will continue to trick them. I can't add sex to this situation. I have to walk away from this, Joshua. I have to walk away and not feel like I lost myself. I can't face the idea that I might finally sort out the money, where I'm going to live, how I'll survive…and lose the only thing I've always had. Myself. I just can't."

He had never begged a woman in his life, but he realized right then that he was on the verge of begging her to agree that it would feel good enough for whatever consequences to be damned. But as he looked behind her at the crib—the crib with the woman's baby in it, for heaven's sake—he realized the argument wasn't going to work with her.

She had been badly used, and though she had never really given him details, the evidence was obvious. She was alone. She had been abandoned at her most vulnerable. For her, the deepest consequences of sex were not hypothetical.

Though, they weren't for him either. And he was a stickler for safe sex, so there was that. Still, he couldn't blame her for not trusting him. And he should want nothing more than to find a woman who was less complicated. One who didn't have all the baggage that Danielle carried.

Still, he wanted to beg.

But he didn't.

"Sex isn't that big of a deal for me," he said. "If you're not into it, that's fine."

She nodded, the gesture jerky. "Good. That's probably another reason we shouldn't."

"I'm going to start interviewing nannies tomorrow," he said, abruptly changing the subject, because if he didn't, he would haul her back into his arms and finish what he had started.

"Okay," she said, looking shell-shocked.

"You'll have a little bit more freedom then. And we can go out riding."

She blinked. "Why? I just turned you down. Why do you want to do anything for me?"

"I already told you. None of this is a trade for sex. You turning me down doesn't change my intentions."

She frowned. "I don't understand." She looked down, picking at her thumbnail. "Everything has a price. There's no reason for you to do something for me when you're not looking for something in return."

"Not everything in life is a transaction, Danielle."

"I suppose it's not when you care about somebody." She tilted her head to the side. "But nobody's ever really cared about me."

If he hadn't already felt like an ass, then her words would have done it. Because his family did care about him. His life had been filled with people doing things for him just because they wanted to give him something. They'd had no expectation of receiving anything in return.

But after Shannon, something had changed inside of him. He wanted to hold everybody at arm's length. Explaining himself felt impossible.

He hadn't wanted to give to anyone, connect with anyone, in a long time. But for some reason, he wanted to connect with Danielle. Wanted to give to that fragile, sweet girl.

It wasn't altruistic. Not really. She had so little that it was easy to step in and do something life altering. She didn't understand the smallest gesture of kindness, which meant the smallest gesture was enough.

"Tomorrow the interview process starts. I assume you want input?"

"Do I want input over who is going to be watching my baby? Yeah. That would be good."

She reached up, absently touching her lips, then lowered her hand quickly, wiggling her fingers slightly. "Good night," she said, the words coming out in a rush.

"Good night," he said, his voice hard. He turned, closing the door resolutely behind him, because if he didn't, he couldn't be responsible for what he might do.

He was going to leave her alone. He was going to do something nice for her. As if that would do something for his tarnished soul.

Well, maybe it wouldn't. But maybe it would do something for her. And for some reason, that mattered.

Maybe that meant he wasn't too far gone after all.

Danielle had never interviewed anyone who was going to work for her. She had interviewed for several jobs herself, but she had never been on the reverse side. It was strange and infused her with an inordinate sense of power.

Which was nice, considering she rarely felt powerful.

Certainly not the other night when Joshua had kissed her. Then she had felt weak as a kitten. Ready to lie down and give him whatever he wanted.

Except she hadn't. She had said no. She was proud of herself for that, even while she mourned the loss of whatever pleasure she might have found with him.

It wasn't about pleasure. It was about pride.

Pride and self-preservation. What she had said to him had been true. If she walked away from this situation completely broken, unable to extricate herself from him, from his life, because she had allowed herself to get tangled up in ways she hadn't anticipated, then she would never forgive herself. If she had finally made her life easier in all the ways she'd always dreamed of, only to snare herself in a trap she knew would end in pain…

She would judge herself harshly for that.

Whatever she wanted to tell herself about Joshua—he was a tool, he didn't deserve the wonderful family he had—she was starting to feel things for him. Things she really couldn't afford to feel.

That story about his girlfriend had hit her hard and deep. Hit her in a place she normally kept well protected.

Dammit.

She took a deep breath and looked over at the new nanny, Janine, who had just started today, and who was going to watch Riley while Joshua and Danielle went for a ride.

She was nervous. Unsteady about leaving Riley for the first time in a while. Necessity had meant she'd had to leave him when she was working at the grocery store. Still, this felt different. Because it wasn't necessary. It made her feel guilty. Because she was leaving him to do something for herself.

She shook her head. Her reaction was ridiculous. But she supposed it was preferable to how her mother had operated. Which was to never think about her children at all. Her neglect of Danielle hadn't come close to her disinterest in her youngest child. Danielle supposed that by the time Riley was born, her mother had been fully burned-out. Had exhausted whatever maternal instinct she'd possessed.

Danielle shook her head. Then took a deep breath and turned to face Janine. "He should nap most of the time we're gone. And even if he wakes up, he's usually really happy."

Janine smiled. "He's just a baby. I've watched a lot of babies. Not that he isn't special," she said, as though she were trying to cover up some faux pas. "I just mean, I'm confident that I can handle him."

Danielle took a deep breath and nodded. Then Joshua came into the room and the breath she had just drawn into her lungs rushed out.

He was wearing a dark blue button-down shirt and jeans, paired with a white cowboy hat that made him look like the hero in an old Western movie.

Do not get that stupid. He might be a hero, but he's not your hero.

No. Girls like her didn't get heroes. They had to be their own heroes. And that was fine. Honestly, it was.

If only she could tell her heart that. Her stupid heart, which was beating out of control.

It was far too easy to remember what it had been like to kiss him. To remember what it had felt like when his stubble-covered cheek scraped against hers. How sexy it had felt. How intoxicating it had been to touch a man like that. To experience the differences between men and women for the first time.

It was dangerous, was what it was. She had opened a door she had never intended to open, and now it was hard to close.

She shook her hands out, then balled them into fists, trying to banish the jitters that were racing through her veins.

"Are you ready?" he asked.

His eyes met hers and all she could think was

how incredible it was that his eyes matched his shirt. They were a deep, perfect shade of navy.

There was something wrong with her. She had never been this stupid around a man before.

"Yes," she said, the answer coming out more as a squeak than an actual word. "I'm ready."

The corner of his mouth lifted into a lopsided grin. "You don't have to be nervous. I'll be gentle with you."

She nearly choked. "Good to know. But I'm more worried about the horse being gentle with me."

"She will be. Promise. I've never taught a girl how to ride before, but I'm pretty confident I can teach you."

His words ricocheted around inside of her, reaching the level of double entendre. Which wasn't fair. That wasn't how he'd meant it.

Or maybe it was.

He hadn't been shy about letting her know exactly what he wanted from her that night. He had put his hand between her legs. Touched her where no other man ever had. He'd made her see stars, tracked sparks over her skin.

It was understandable for her to be affected by the experience. But like he'd said, sex didn't really matter to him. It wasn't a big deal. So why he would be thinking of it now was beyond her. He had probably forgotten already. Probably that kiss had become an indistinct blur in his mind, mixed with all his other sexual encounters.

There were no other encounters for her. So there he was in her mind, and in front of her, far too sharp and far too clear.

"I'm ready," she said, the words rushed. "Totally ready."

"Great," he said. "Let's go."

Taking Danielle out riding was submitting himself to a particular kind of torture, that was for sure. But he was kind of into punishing himself… so he figured it fit his MO.

He hadn't stopped thinking about her since they had kissed—and more—in her bedroom the other night. He had done his best to throw himself into work, to avoid her, but still, he kept waking up with sweat slicked over his skin, his cock hard and dreams of…her lips, her tongue, her scent… lingering in his thoughts.

Normally, the outdoors cleared his mind. Riding his horse along the length of the property was his therapy. Maneuvering her over the rolling hills, along the ridge line of the mountain, the evergreen trees rising behind them in a stately backdrop that left him feeling small within the greater context of the world. Which was something a man like him found refreshing some days.

But not today.

Today, he was obsessing. He was watching Danielle's ass as she rode her horse in front of him, the motion of the horse's gait making him think of what it would look like if the woman was riding him instead of his mare.

He couldn't understand this. Couldn't understand this obsession with her.

She wasn't the kind of sophisticated woman he tended to favor. In a lot of ways, she reminded him of the kind of girl he used to go for here in town, back when he had been a good-for-nothing teenager spending his free time drinking and getting laid out in the woods.

Back then he had liked hometown girls who wanted the same things he did. A few hours to escape, a little bit of fun.

The problem was, he already knew Danielle didn't want that. She didn't find casual hookups fun. And he didn't have anything to offer beyond a casual hookup.

The other problem was that the feelings he had for her were not casual. If they were, then he wouldn't be obsessing. But he was.

In the couple of weeks since she had come to live with him, she had started to fill out a bit. He could get a sense of her figure, of how she would look if she were thriving rather than simply surviving. She was naturally thin, but there was something elegant about her curves.

But even more appealing than the baser things, like the perky curve of her high breasts and the subtle slope of her hips, was the stubborn set of her jaw. The straight, brittle weight of her shoulders spoke of both strength and fragility.

While there was something unbreakable about her, he worried that if a man ever were to find her weakness, she would do more than just break. She would shatter.

He shook his head. And then he forced himself to look away from her, forced himself to look at the scenery. At the mountain spread out before them, and the ocean gray and fierce behind it.

"Am I doing okay?"

Danielle's question made it impossible to ignore her, and he found himself looking at her ass again. "You haven't fallen off yet," he said, perhaps a bit unkindly.

She snorted, then looked over her shoulder, a challenging light glittering in her brown eyes. "Yet? I'm not going to fall off, Joshua Grayson. It would take a hell of a lot to unseat me."

"Says the woman who was shaking when I helped her mount up earlier."

She surprised him by releasing her hold on the reins with one hand and waving it in the air. "Well, I'm getting the hang of it."

"You're a regular cowgirl," he said.

Suddenly, he wanted that to be true. It was the

strangest thing. He wanted her to have this outlet, this freedom. Something more than a small apartment. Something more than struggle.

You're giving her that. That's what this entire bargain is for. Like she said, she's a gold digger, and you're giving her your gold.

Yes, but he wanted to give her more than that.

Just like he had told her the other day, what he wanted to give her wasn't about an exchange. He wanted her to have something for herself. Something for Riley.

Maybe it was a misguided attempt to atone for what he hadn't managed to give Shannon. What he hadn't ever been able to give the child he lost.

He swallowed hard, taking in a deep breath of the sharp pine and salt air, trying to ease the pressure in his chest.

She looked at him again, this time a dazzling smile on her lips. It took all that pressure in his chest and punched a hole right through it. He felt his lungs expand, all of him begin to expand.

He clenched his teeth, grinding them together so hard he was pretty sure his jaw was going to break. "Are you about ready to head back?"

"No. But I'm not sure I'm ever going to be ready to head back. This was… Thank you." She didn't look at him this time. But he had a feeling it was because she was a lot less comfortable with sincere connection than she was with sarcasm.

Well, that made two of them.

"You're welcome," he said, fixing his gaze on the line of trees beside them.

He maneuvered his horse around in front of hers so he could lead the way back down to the barn. They rode on in silence, but he could feel her staring holes into his back.

"Are you looking at my butt, Danielle?"

He heard a sputtering noise behind him. "No."

They rode up to the front of the barn and he dismounted, then walked over to her horse. "Liar. Do you need help?"

She frowned, her brows lowering. "Not from you. You called me a liar."

"Because you were looking at my ass and we both know it." He raised his hand up, extending it to her. "Now let me help you so you don't fall on your pretty face."

"Bah," she said, reaching out to him, her fingers brushing against his, sending an electrical current arcing between them. He chose to ignore it. Because there was no way in the whole damn world that the brush of a woman's fingertips against his should get him hot and bothered.

He grabbed hold of her and helped get her down from the horse, drawing her against him when her feet connected with the ground. And then it was over.

Pretending that this wasn't a long prelude to him

kissing her again. Pretending that the last few days hadn't been foreplay. Pretending that every time either of them had thought about the kiss hadn't been easing them closer and closer to the inevitable.

She wanted him, he knew that. It was clear in the way she responded to him. She might have reservations about acting on it, and he had his own. But need was bigger than any of that right now, building between them, impossible to ignore.

He was a breath away from claiming her mouth with his when she shocked him by curving her fingers around his neck and stretching up on her toes.

Her kiss was soft, tentative. A question where his kiss would have been a command. But that made it all the sweeter. The fact that she had come to him. The fact that even though she was still conflicted about all of it, she couldn't resist any longer.

He cupped her cheek, calling on all his restraint—what little there was—to allow her to lead this, to allow her to guide the exploration. There was something so unpracticed about that pretty mouth of hers, something untutored about the way her lips skimmed over his. About the almost sweet, soft way her tongue tested his.

What he wanted to do was take it deep. Take it hard. What he wanted to do was grab hold of her hips and press her back against the barn. Push her jeans down her thighs and get his hand back between her gorgeous legs so he could feel all that soft, slick flesh.

What he wanted was to press his cock against her entrance and slide in slowly, savoring the feel of her desire as it washed over him.

But he didn't.

And it was the damned hardest thing he had ever done. To wait. To let her lead. To let her believe she had the control here. Whatever she needed to do so she wouldn't get scared again. If he had to be patient, if he had to take it slow, he could. He would.

If it meant having her.

He had to have her. Had to exorcise the intense demon that had taken residence inside of him, that demanded he take her. Demanded he make her his own.

His horse snickered behind them, shifting her bulk, drawing Danielle's focus back to the present and away from him. Dammit all.

"Let me get them put away," he said.

He was going to do it quickly. And then he was going to get right back to tasting her. He half expected her to run to the house as he removed the tack from the animals and got them brushed down, but she didn't. Instead, she just stood there watching him, her eyes large, her expression one of absolute indecision.

Because she knew.

She knew that if she stayed down here, he wasn't going to leave it at a kiss. He wasn't going to leave it at all.

But he went about his tasks, slowing his movements, forcing himself not to rush. Forcing himself to draw it out. For her torture as well as his. He wanted her to need it, the way that he did.

And yes, he could see she wanted to run. He could also tell she wanted him, she wanted this. She was unbearably curious, even if she was also afraid.

And he was counting on that curiosity to win out.

Finally, she cleared her throat, shifting impatiently. "Are you going to take all day to do that?"

"You have to take good care of your horses, Danielle. I know a city girl like you doesn't understand how that works."

She squinted, then took a step forward, pulling his hat off his head and depositing it on her own. "Bullshit. You're playing with me."

He couldn't hold back the smile. "Not yet. But I plan to."

After that, he hurried a bit. He put the horses back in their paddock, then took hold of Danielle's hand, leading her deeper into the barn, to a ladder that went up to the loft.

"Can I show you something?"

She bit her lip, hesitating. "Why do I have a feeling that it isn't the loft you're going to show me?"

"I'm going to show you the loft. It's just not all I'm going to show you."

She took a step back, worrying her lip with her teeth. He reached out, cupping the back of her head and bringing his mouth down on hers, kissing her the way he had wanted to when she initiated the kiss outside. He didn't have patience anymore. And he wasn't going to let her lead. Not now.

He cupped her face, stroking her cheeks with his thumbs. "This has nothing to do with our agreement. It has nothing to do with the contract. Nothing to do with the ad or my father or anything other than the fact that I want you. Do you understand?"

She nodded slowly. "Yes," she said, the word coming out a whisper.

Adrenaline shot through him, a strange kind of triumph that came with a kick to the gut right behind it. He wanted her. He knew he didn't deserve her. But he wasn't going to stop himself from having her in spite of that.

Then he took her hand and led her up the ladder.

Seven

Danielle's heart was pounding in her ears. It was all she could hear. The sound of her own heart beating as she climbed the rungs that led up to the loft.

It was different than she had imagined. It was clean. There was a haystack in one corner, but beyond that the floor was immaculate, every item stored and organized with precision. Which, knowing Joshua like she now did, wasn't too much of a surprise.

That made her smile, just a little. She did know him. In some ways, she felt like she knew him better than she knew anyone.

She wasn't sure what that said about her other relationships. For a while, she'd had friends, but they'd disappeared when she'd become consumed with caring for her pregnant mother and working as much as possible at the grocery store. And then no one had come back when Danielle ended up with full care of Riley.

In some ways, she didn't blame them. Life was hard enough without dealing with a friend who was juggling all of that. But just because she understood didn't mean she wasn't lonely.

She looked at Joshua, their eyes connecting. He had shared his past with her. But she was keeping something big from him. Even while she was prepared to give him her body, she was holding back secrets.

She took a breath, opening her mouth to speak, but something in his blue gaze stopped the words before they could form. Something sharp, predatory. Something that made her feel like she was the center of the world, or at least the center of his world.

It was intoxicating. She'd never experienced it before.

She wanted more, all of it. Wherever it would lead.

And that was scary. Scarier than agreeing to do something she had never done before. Because she finally understood. Understood why her mother had traded her sanity, and her self-worth, for that moment when a man looked at you like you were his everything.

Danielle had spent so long being nothing to anyone. Nothing but a burden. Now, feeling like the solution rather than the problem was powerful, heady. She knew she couldn't turn back now no matter what.

Even if sanity tried to prevail, she would shove it aside. Because she needed this. Needed this balm for all the wounds that ran so deep inside of her.

Joshua walked across the immaculate space and opened up a cabinet. There were blankets inside, thick, woolen ones with geometric designs on them. He pulled out two and spread one on the ground.

She bit her lip, fighting a rising tide of hysteria, fighting a giggle that was climbing its way up her throat.

"I know this isn't exactly a fancy hotel suite."

She forced a smile. "It works for me."

He set the other blanket down on the end of the first one, still folded, then he reached out and took her hand, drawing her to him. He curved his fingers around her wrist, lifting her arm up, then shifted his hold, lacing his fingers through hers and dipping his head, pressing his lips to her own.

Her heart was still pounding that same, steady

beat, and she was certain he must be able to hear it. Must be aware of just how he was affecting her.

There were all sorts of things she should tell him. About Riley's mother. About this being her first time.

But she didn't have the words.

She had her heartbeat. The way her limbs trembled. She could let him see that her eyes were filling with tears, and no matter how fiercely she blinked, they never quite went away.

She was good at manipulating conversation. At giving answers that walked the line between fact and fiction.

Her body could only tell the truth.

She hoped he could see it. That he understood. Later, they would talk. Later, there would be honesty between them. Because he would have questions. God knew. But for now, she would let the way her fingertips trailed down his back— uncertain and tentative—the way she peppered kisses along his jaw—clumsy and broken—say everything she couldn't.

"It doesn't need to be fancy," she said, her voice sounding thick even to her own ears.

"Maybe it should be," he said, his voice rough. "But if I was going to take you back to my bedroom, I expect I would have to wait until tonight. And I don't want to wait."

She shook her head. "It doesn't have to be fancy. It just has to be now. And it has to be you."

He drew his head back, inhaling sharply. And then he cupped her cheek and consumed her. His kiss was heat and fire, sparking against the dry, neglected things inside her and raging out of control.

She slid her hands up his arms, hanging on to his strong shoulders, using his steadiness to hold her fast even as her legs turned weak.

He lifted her up against him, then swept his arm beneath her legs, cradling her against his chest like she was a child. Then he set her down gently on the blanket, continuing to kiss her as he did so.

She was overwhelmed. Overwhelmed by the intensity of his gaze, by his focus. Overwhelmed by his closeness, his scent.

He was everywhere. His hands on her body, his face filling her vision.

She had spent the past few months caring for her half brother, pouring everything she had onto one little person she loved more than anything in the entire world. But in doing so, she had left herself empty. She had been giving continually, opening a vein and bleeding whenever necessary, and taking nothing in to refill herself.

But this… This was more than she had ever had. More than she'd ever thought she could have. Being the focus of a man's attention. Of his need.

This was a different kind of need than that of a

child. Because it wasn't entirely selfish. Joshua's need gave her something in return; it compelled him to be close. Compelled him to kiss her, to skim his hands over her body, teasing and tormenting her with the promise of a pleasure she had never experienced.

Before she could think her actions through, she was pushing her fingertips beneath the hem of his shirt, his hard, flat stomach hot to the touch. And then it didn't matter what she had done before or what she hadn't done. Didn't matter that she was a virgin and this was an entirely new experience.

Need replaced everything except being skin to skin with him. Having nothing between them.

Suddenly, the years of feeling isolated, alone, cold and separate were simply too much. She needed his body over hers, his body inside hers. Whatever happened after that, whatever happened in the end, right now she couldn't care.

Because her desire outweighed the consequences. A wild, desperate thing starving to be fed. With his touch. With his possession.

She pushed his shirt up, and he helped her shrug it over his head. Her throat dried, her mouth opening slightly as she looked at him. His shoulders were broad, his chest well-defined and muscular, pale hair spreading over those glorious muscles, down his ridged abdomen, disappearing in a thin trail beneath the waistband of his low-slung jeans.

She had never seen a man who looked like him before, not in person. And she had never been this close to a man ever. She pressed her palm against his chest, relishing his heat and his hardness beneath her touch. His heart raging out of control, matching the beat of her own.

She parted her thighs and he settled between them. She could feel the hard ridge of his arousal pressing against that place where she was wet and needy for him. She was shocked at how hard he was, even through layers of clothing.

And she lost herself in his kiss, in the way he rocked his hips against hers. This moment, this experience was like everything she had missed growing up. Misspent teenage years when she should have been making out with boys in barns and hoping she didn't get caught. In reality, her mother wouldn't have cared.

This was a reclamation. More than that, it was something completely new. Something she had never even known she could want.

Joshua was something she had never known she could want.

It shouldn't make sense, the two of them. This brilliant businessman in his thirties who owned a ranch and seemed to shun most emotional connections. And her. Poor. In her twenties. Desperately clinging to any connection she could forge because each one was so rare and special.

But somehow they seemed to make sense. Kissing each other. Touching each other. For some reason, he was the only man that made sense.

Maybe it was because he had taught her to ride a horse. Maybe it was because he was giving her and Riley a ticket out of poverty. Maybe it was because he was handsome. She had a feeling this connection transcended all those things.

As his tongue traced a trail down her neck to the collar of her T-shirt, she was okay with not knowing. She didn't need to give this connection a name. She didn't even want to.

Her breath caught as he pushed her shirt up and over her head, then quickly dispensed with her bra using a skill not even she possessed. Her nipples tightened, and she was painfully aware of them and of the fact that she was a little lackluster in size.

If Joshua noticed, he didn't seem to mind.

Instead, he dipped his head, sucking one tightened bud between his lips. The move was so sudden, so shocking and so damned unexpected that she couldn't stop herself from arching into him, a cry on her lips.

He looked up, the smile on his face so damned cocky she should probably have been irritated. But she wasn't. She just allowed herself to get lost. In his heat. In the fire that flared between them. In the way he used his lips, his teeth and his tongue to draw a map of pleasure over her skin. All the way down to the waistband of her pants. He licked her. Just above the snap on her jeans. Another sensation so deliciously shocking she couldn't hold back the sound of pleasure on her lips.

She pressed her fist against her mouth, trying to keep herself from getting too vocal. From embarrassing herself. From revealing just how inexperienced she was. The noises she was making definitely announced the fact that these sensations were revelatory to her. And that made her feel a touch too vulnerable.

She was so used to holding people at a distance. So used to benign neglect and general apathy creating a shield around her feelings. Her secrets.

But there was no distance here.

And certainly none as he undid the button of her jeans and drew the zipper down slowly. As he pushed the rough denim down her legs, taking her panties with them.

If she had felt vulnerable a moment before, that was nothing compared to now. She felt so fragile. So exposed. And then he reached up, pressing his hand against her leg at the inside of her knee, spreading her wide so he could look his fill.

She wanted to snap her legs together. Wanted to cover up. But she was immobilized. Completely captive to whatever might happen next. She was so desperate to find out, and at the same time desperate to escape it.

Rough fingertips drifted down the tender skin on her inner thigh, brushing perilously close to her damp, needy flesh. And then he was there. His touch in no way gentle or tentative as he pressed his hand against her, the heel of his palm putting firm pressure on her clit before he pressed his fingers down and spread her wide.

He made his intentions clear as he lowered his head, tasting her deeply. She lifted her hips, a sharp sound on her lips, one she didn't even bother to hold back. He shifted his hold, gripping her hips, holding her just wide enough for his broad shoulders to fit right there, his sensual assault merciless.

Tension knotted her stomach like a fist, tighter and tighter with each pass of his tongue. Then he pressed his thumb against her clit at the same time as he flicked his tongue against that sensitive bundle of nerves. She grabbed hold of him, her fingernails digging into his back.

He drew his thumb down her crease, teasing the entrance of her body. She rocked her hips with the motion, desperate for something. Feeling suddenly empty and achy and needy in ways she never had before.

He rotated his hand, pressing his middle finger deep inside of her, and she gasped at the foreign invasion. But any discomfort passed quickly as her body grew wetter beneath the ministrations of his tongue. By the time he added a second finger, it slipped in easily.

He quickened his pace, and it felt like there was an earthquake starting inside her. A low, slow pull at her core that spread outward, her limbs trembling as the pressure at her center continued to mount.

His thumb joined with his tongue as he continued to pump his fingers inside her, and it was that added pressure that finally broke her. She was shaken. Rattled completely. The magnitude of measurable aftershocks rocking her long after the primary force had passed.

He moved into a sitting position, undoing his belt and the button on his jeans. Then he stood for a moment, drawing the zipper down slowly and pushing the denim down his muscular thighs.

She had never seen a naked man in person before, and the stark, thick evidence of his arousal standing out from his body was a clear reminder that they weren't finished, no matter how wrung out and replete she felt.

Except, even though she felt satisfied, limp from the intensity of her release, she did want more. Because there was more to have. Because she wanted to be close to him. Because she wanted to give him even an ounce of the satisfaction that she had just experienced.

He knelt back down, pulling his jeans closer and taking his wallet out of his back pocket. He produced a condom packet and she gave thanks for his presence of mind. She knew better than to have unprotected sex with someone. For myriad reasons. But still, she wondered if she would have remembered if he had not.

Thank God one of them was thinking. She was too overwhelmed. Too swamped by the release that had overtaken her, and by the enormity of what was about to happen. When he positioned himself at the entrance of her body and pressed the thick head of his cock against her, she gasped in shock.

It *hurt*. Dear God it hurt. His fingers hadn't prepared her for the rest of him.

He noticed her hesitation and slowed his movements, pressing inside her inch by excruciating inch. She held on to his shoulders, closing her eyes and burying her face in his neck as he jerked his hips forward, fully seating himself inside her.

She did her best to breathe through it. But she was in a daze. Joshua was inside her, and she wasn't a virgin anymore. It felt… Well, it didn't feel like losing anything. It felt like gaining something. Gaining a whole lot.

The pain began to recede and she looked up, at his face, at the extreme concentration there, at the set of his jaw, the veins in his neck standing out.

"Are you okay?" he asked, his voice strangled.

She nodded wordlessly, then flexed her hips experimentally.

He groaned, lowering his head, pressing his forehead against hers, before kissing her. Then he began to move.

Soon, that same sweet tension began to build again in her stomach, need replacing the bone-deep satisfaction that she had only just experienced. She didn't know how it was possible to be back in that needy place only moments after feeling fulfilled.

But she was. And then she was lost in the rhythm, lost in the feeling of his thick length stroking in and out of her, all of the pain gone now, only pleasure remaining. It was so foreign, so singular and unlike anything she had ever experienced. And she loved it. Reveled in it.

But even more than her own pleasure, she reveled in watching his unraveling.

Because he had pulled her apart in a million astounding ways, and she didn't know if she could ever be reassembled. So it was only fair that he lost himself too. Only fair that she be his undoing in some way.

Sweat beaded on his brow, trickled down his back. She reveled in the feel of it beneath her fingertips. In the obvious evidence of what this did to him.

His breathing became more labored, his muscles shaking as each thrust became less gentle. As he began to pound into her. And just as he needed to go harder, go faster, so did she.

Her own pleasure wound around his, inextricably linked.

On a harsh growl he buried his face in her neck, his arms shaking as he thrust into her one last time, slamming into her clit, breaking a wave of pleasure over her body as he found his own release.

He tried to pull away, but she wrapped her arms around him, holding him close. Because the sooner he separated from her body, the sooner they would have to talk. And she wasn't exactly sure she wanted to talk.

But when he lifted his head, his blue eyes glinting in the dim light, she could tell that whether or not she wanted to talk, they were going to.

He rolled away from her, pushing into a sitting position. "Are you going to explain all of this to me? Or are you going to make me guess?"

"What?" She sounded overly innocent, her eyes wider than necessary.

"Danielle, I'm going to ask you a question, and I need you to answer me honestly. Were you a virgin?"

Joshua's blood was still running hot through his veins, arousal still burning beneath the surface of his skin. And he knew the question he had just asked her was probably insane. He could explain her discomfort as pain because she hadn't taken a man to her bed since she'd given birth.

But that wasn't it. It wasn't.

The more credence he gave to his virgin theory, the more everything about her started to make sense. The way she responded to his kiss, the way she acted when he touched her.

Her reaction had been about more than simple attraction, more than pleasure. There had been wonder there. A sense of discovery.

But that meant Riley wasn't her son. And it meant she had been fucking lying to him.

"Well, Joshua, given that this is not a New Testament kind of situation…"

He reached out, grabbing hold of her wrist and tugging her upward, drawing her toward him. "Don't lie to me."

"Why would you think that?" she asked, her words small. Admission enough as far as he was concerned.

"A lot of reasons. But I have had sex with a virgin before. More accurately, Sadie Miller and I took each other's virginity in the woods some eighteen years ago. You don't forget that. And, I grant you, there could be other reasons for the fact that it hurt you, for the fact that you were tight." A flush spread over her skin, her cheeks turning beet red. "But I don't think any of those reasons are the truth. So what's going on? Who is Riley's mother?"

A tear slid down her cheek, her expression mutinous and angry. "I am," she said, her voice trembling. "At least, I might as well be. I should be."

"You didn't give birth to Riley."

She sniffed loudly, another tear sliding down her cheek. "No. I didn't."

"Are you running from somebody? Is there something I need to know?"

"It's not like that. I'm not hiding. I didn't steal him. I have legal custody of Riley. But my situation was problematic. At least, as far as Child Services was concerned. I lost my job because of the baby-sitting situation and I needed money."

She suddenly looked so incredibly young, so vulnerable... And he felt like the biggest prick on planet Earth.

She had lied to him. She had most definitely led him to believe she was in an entirely different circumstance than she was, and still, he was mostly angry at himself.

Because the picture she was painting was even more desperate than the one he had been led to believe. Because she had been a virgin and he had just roughly dispensed with that.

She had been desperate. Utterly desperate. And had taken this post with him because she hadn't seen another option. Whatever he'd thought of her before, he was forced to revise it, and there was no way that revision didn't include recasting himself as the villain.

"Whose baby is he?"

She swallowed hard, drawing her knees up to her chest, covering her nudity. "Riley is my half brother. My mother showed up at my place about a year ago pregnant and desperate. She needed someone to help her out. When she came to me, she sounded pretty determined to take care of him. She even named him. She told me she would do better for him than she had for me, because she was done with men now and all of that. But she broke her promises. She had the baby, she met somebody else. I didn't know it at first. I didn't realize she was leaving Riley in the apartment alone sometimes while I was at work."

She took a deep, shuddering breath, then continued. "I didn't mess around when I found out. I didn't wait for her to decide to abandon him. I called Child Services. And I got temporary guardianship. My mother left. But then things started to fall apart with the work, and I didn't know how I was going to pay for the apartment... Then I saw your ad."

He swore. "You should have told me."

"Maybe. But I needed the money, Joshua. And I didn't want to do anything to jeopardize your offer. I could tell you were uncomfortable that I brought a baby with me, and now I know why. But, regardless, at the time, I didn't want to do anything that might compromise our arrangement."

He felt like the ass he undoubtedly was. The worst part was, it shone a light on all the bullshit he'd put her through. Regardless of Riley's parentage, she'd been desperate and he'd taken advantage of that. Less so when he'd been keeping his hands to himself. At least then it had been feasible to pretend it was an even exchange.

But now?

Now he'd slept with her and it was impossible to keep pretending.

And frankly, he didn't want to.

He'd been wrestling with this feeling from the moment they'd gone out riding today, or maybe since they'd left his parents' house last week.

But today…when he'd looked at her, seen her smile…noticed the way she'd gained weight after being in a place where she felt secure…

He'd wanted to give her more of that.

He'd wanted to do more good than harm. Had wanted to fix something instead of break it.

It was too late for Shannon. But he could help Danielle. He could make sure she always felt safe. That she and Riley were always protected.

The realization would have made him want to laugh if it didn't all feel too damned grim. Somehow his father's ad had brought him to this place when he'd been determined to teach the old man a lesson.

But Joshua hadn't counted on Danielle.

Hadn't counted on how she would make him feel. That she'd wake something inside him he'd thought had been asleep for good.

It wasn't just chemistry. Wasn't just sex. It was the desire to make her happy. To give her things.

To fix what was broken.

He knew the solution wouldn't come from him personally, but his money could sure as hell fix her problems. And they did have chemistry. The kind that wasn't common. It sure as hell went beyond anything he'd ever experienced before.

"The truth doesn't change anything," she said, lowering her face into her arms, her words muffled. "It doesn't."

He reached out, taking her chin between his thumb and forefinger, tilting her face back up. "It does. Even if it shouldn't. Though, maybe it's not Riley that changes it. Maybe it's just the two of us."

She shook her head. "It doesn't have to change anything."

"Danielle… I can't…"

She lurched forward, grabbing his arm, her eyes wide, her expression wild. "Joshua, please. I need this money. I can't go back to where we were. I'm being held to a harsher standard than his biological mother would be and I can't lose him."

He grabbed her chin again, steadying her face, looking into those glistening brown eyes. "Danielle, I would never let you lose him. I want to protect you. Both of you."

She tilted her head to the side, her expression growing suspicious. "You…do?"

"I've been thinking. I was thinking this earlier when we were riding, but now, knowing your whole story…I want you and Riley to stay with me."

She blinked. "What?"

"Danielle, I want you to marry me."

Eight

Danielle couldn't process any of this.

She had expected him to be angry. Had expected him to get mad because she'd lied to him.

She hadn't expected a marriage proposal.

At least, she was pretty sure that was what had just happened. "You want to…marry me? For real marry me?"

"Yes," he said, his tone hard, decisive. "You don't feel good about fooling my family—neither do I. You need money and security and, hell, I have both. We have chemistry. I want… I don't want to send you back into the world alone. You don't even know where you're going."

He wasn't wrong. And dammit his offer was tempting. They were both naked, and he was so beautiful, and she wanted to kiss him again. Touch him again. But more than that, she wanted him to hold her in his arms again.

She wanted to be close to him. Bonded to him.

She wanted—so desperately—to not be alone.

But there had to be a catch.

There was always a catch. He could say whatever he wanted about how all of this wasn't a transaction, how he had taken her riding just to take her riding. But then they'd had sex. And he'd had a condom in his wallet.

So he'd been prepared.

That made her stomach sour.

"Did you plan this?" she asked. "The horse-riding seduction?"

"No, I didn't plan it. I carry a condom because I like to be prepared to have sex. You never know. You can get mad at me for that if you want, but then, we did need one, so it seems a little hypocritical."

"Are you tricking me?" she asked, feeling desperate and panicky. "Is this a trick? Because I don't understand how it benefits you to marry me. To keep Riley and me here. You don't even like Riley, Joshua. You can't stand to be in the same room with him."

"I broke Shannon," he said, his voice hard. "I

ruined her. I did that. But I won't break you. I want
to fix this."

"You can't slap duct tape and a wedding band
on me and call it done," she said, her voice trembling. "I'm not a leaky faucet."

"I didn't say you were. But you need something
I have and I… Danielle, I need you." His voice was
rough, intense. "I'm not offering you love, but I
can be faithful. I was ready to be a husband years
ago, that part doesn't faze me. I can take care of
you. I can keep you safe. And if I send you out
into the world with nothing more than money and
something happens to you or Riley, I won't forgive
myself. So stay with me. Marry me."

It was crazy. He was crazy.

And she was crazy for sitting there fully considering everything he was offering.

But she was imagining a life here. For her, for
Riley. On Joshua's ranch, in his beautiful house.

And she knew—she absolutely knew—that
what she had felt physically with him, what had
just happened, was a huge reason why they were
having this conversation at all.

More than the pleasure, the closeness drew her
in. Actually, that was the most dangerous part of
his offer. The idea that she could go through life
with somebody by her side. To raise Riley with
this strong man backing her up.

Something clenched tight in her chest, working

its way down to her stomach. Riley. He could have a father figure. She didn't know exactly what function Joshua would play in his life. Joshua had trouble with the baby right now. But she knew Joshua was a good man, and that he would never freeze Riley out intentionally. Not when he was offering them a life together.

"What about Riley?" she asked, her throat dry. She swallowed hard. She had to know what he was thinking.

"What about him?"

"This offer extends to him too. And I mean… not just protection and support. But would you… Would you teach him things? Would your father be a grandfather to him? Would your brothers be uncles and your sister be an aunt? I understand that having a child around might be hard for you, after you lost your chance at being a father. And I understand you want to fix me, my situation. And it's tempting, Joshua, it's very tempting. But I need to know if that support, if all of that, extends to Riley."

Joshua's face looked as though it had been cast in stone. "I'm not sure if I would be a good father, Danielle. I was going to be a father, and so I was going to figure it out—how to do that, how to be that. I suppose I can apply that same intent here. I can't guarantee that I'll be the best, but I'll try.

And you're right. I have my family to back me up. And he has you."

That was it.

That was the reason she couldn't say no. Because if she walked away from Joshua now, Riley would have her. Only her. She loved him, but she was just one person. If she stayed here with Joshua, Riley would have grandparents. Aunts and uncles. Family. People who knew how to be a family. She was doing the very best she could, but her idea of family was somewhere between cold neglectful nightmare and a TV sitcom.

The Grayson family knew—Joshua knew— what it meant to be a family. If she said yes, she could give that to Riley.

She swallowed again, trying to alleviate the scratchy feeling in her throat.

"I guess… I guess I can't really say no to that." She straightened, still naked, and not even a little bit embarrassed. There were bigger things going on here than the fact that he could see her breasts. "Okay, Joshua. I'll marry you."

Nine

The biggest problem with this sudden change in plan was the fact that Joshua had deliberately set out to make his family dislike Danielle. And now he was marrying her for real.

Of course, the flaw in his original plan was that Danielle *hadn't* been roundly hated by his family. They'd distrusted the whole situation, certainly, but his family was simply too fair, too nice to hate her.

Still, guilt clutched at him, and he knew he was going to have to do something to fix this. Which was why he found himself down at the Gray Bear Construction office rather than working from home. Because he knew Faith and Isaiah would be in, and he needed to have a talk with his siblings.

The office was a newly constructed building fashioned to look like a log cabin. It was down at the edge of town, by where Rona's diner used to be, a former greasy spoon that had been transformed into a series of smaller, hipper shops that were more in line with the interests of Copper Ridge's tourists.

It was a great office space with a prime view of the ocean, but still, Joshua typically preferred to work in the privacy of his own home, secluded in the mountains.

Isaiah did too, which was why it was notable that his brother was in the office today, but he'd had a meeting of some kind, so he'd put on a decent shirt and a pair of nice jeans and gotten his ass out of his hermitage.

Faith, being the bright, sharp creature she was, always came into the office, always dressed in some variation of her personal uniform. Black pants and a black top—a sweater today because of the chilly weather.

"What are you doing here?" Faith asked, her expression scrutinizing.

"I came here to talk to you," he said.

"I'll make coffee." Joshua turned and saw Poppy standing there. Strange, he hadn't noticed. But then, Poppy usually stayed in the background.

He couldn't remember running the business without her, but like useful office supplies, you really only noticed them when they didn't work. And Poppy always worked.

"Thanks, Poppy," Faith said.

Isaiah folded his arms over his chest and leaned back in his chair. "What's up?"

"I'm getting married in two weeks."

Faith made a scoffing sound. "To that child you're dating?"

"She's your age," he said. "And yes. Just like I said I was."

"Which begs the question," Isaiah said. "Why are you telling us again?"

"Because. The first time I was lying. Dad put that ad in the paper trying to find a wife for me, and I selected Danielle in order to teach him a lesson. The joke's on me it turns out." Damn was it ever.

"Good God, Joshua. You're such an ass," Faith said, leaning against the wall, her arms folded, mirroring Isaiah's stance. "I knew something was up, but of all the things I suspected, you tricking our mother and father was not one of them."

"What did you suspect?"

"That you were thinking with your... Well. And now I'm back to that conclusion. Because why are you marrying her?"

"I care about her. And believe me when I say she's had it rough."

"You've slept with her?" This question came from Isaiah, and there was absolutely no tact in it. But then, Isaiah himself possessed absolutely no tact. Which was why he handled money and not people.

"Yes," Joshua said.

"She must be good. But I'm not sure that's going to convince either of us you're thinking with your big brain." His brother stood up, not unfolding his arms.

"Well, you're an asshole," Joshua returned. "The sex has nothing to do with it. I can get sex whenever I want."

Faith made a hissing sound. He tossed his younger sister a glance. "You can stop hissing and settle down," he said to her. "You were the one who brought sex into it, I'm just clarifying. You know what I went through with Shannon, what I put Shannon through. If I send Danielle and her baby back out into the world and something happens to them, I'll never forgive myself."

"Well, Joshua, that kind of implies you aren't already living in a perpetual state of self-flagellation," Faith said.

"Do you want to see if it can get worse?"

She shook her head. "No, but marrying some random woman you found through an ad seems like an extreme way to go about searching for atonement. Can't you do some Hail Marys or something?"

"If it were that simple, I would have done it a long time ago." He took a deep breath. "I'm not going to tell Mom and Dad the whole story. But I'm telling you because I need you to be nice about Danielle. However it looked when I brought her by to introduce her to the family...I threw her under the bus, and now I want to drag her back out from under it."

Isaiah shook his head. "You're a contrary son of a bitch."

"Well, usually that's your function. I figured it was my turn."

The door to the office opened and in walked their business partner, Jonathan Bear, who ran the construction side of the firm. He looked around the room, clearly confused by the fact that they were all in residence. "Is there a meeting I didn't know about?"

"Joshua is getting married," Faith said, looking sullen.

"Congratulations," Jonathan said, smiling, which was unusual for the other man, who was typically pretty taciturn. "I can highly recommend it."

Jonathan had married the pastor's daughter, Hayley Thompson, in a small ceremony recently.

In the past, Jonathan had walked around like

he had his own personal storm cloud overhead, and since meeting Hayley, he had most definitely changed. Maybe there was something to that whole marriage thing. Maybe Joshua's idea of atonement wasn't as outrageous as it might have initially seemed.

"There," Joshua said. "Jonathan recommends it. So you two can stop looking at me suspiciously."

Jonathan shrugged and walked through the main area and into the back, toward his office, leaving Joshua alone with his siblings.

Faith tucked her hair behind her ear. "Honestly, whatever you need, whatever you want, I'll help. But I don't want you to get hurt."

"And I appreciate that," he said. "But the thing is, you can only get hurt if there's love involved. I don't love her."

Faith looked wounded by that. "Then what's the point? I'm not trying to argue. I just don't understand."

"Love is not the be-all and end-all, Faith. Sometimes just committing to taking care of somebody else is enough. I loved Shannon, but I still didn't do the right thing for her. I'm older now. And I know what's important. I'm going to keep Danielle safe. I'm going to keep Riley safe. What's more important than that?" He shook his head. "I'm sure Shannon would have rather had that than any expression of love."

"Fine," she said. "I support you. I'm in."

"So you aren't going to be a persnickety brat?"

A small smile quirked her lips upward. "I didn't say that. I said I would support you. But as a younger sister, I feel the need to remind you that being a persnickety brat is sometimes part of my support."

He shot Isaiah a baleful look. "I suppose you're still going to be an asshole?"

"Obviously."

Joshua smiled then. Because that was the best he was going to get from his siblings. But it was a step toward making sure Danielle felt like she had a place in the family, rather than feeling like an outsider.

And if he wanted that with an intensity that wasn't strictly normal or healthy, he would ignore that. He had never pretended to be normal or healthy. He wasn't going to start now.

Danielle was getting fluttery waiting for Joshua to come home. The anticipation was a strange feeling. It had been a long time since she'd looked forward to someone coming home. She remembered being young, when it was hard to be alone. But she hadn't exactly wished for her mother to come home, because she knew that when her mother arrived, she would be drunk. And Danielle would be tasked with managing her in some way.

That was the story of her life. Not being alone meant taking care of somebody. Being alone meant isolation, but at least she had time to herself.

But Joshua wasn't like that. Being with him didn't mean she had to manage him.

She thought of their time together in the barn, and the memory made her shiver. She had gone to bed in her own room last night, and he hadn't made any move toward her since his proposal. She had a feeling his hesitation had something to do with her inexperience.

But she was ready for him again. Ready for more.

She shook her hands out, feeling jittery. And a little scared.

It was so easy to want him. To dream about him coming home, how she would embrace him, kiss him. And maybe even learn to cook, so she could make him dinner. Learn to do something other than warm up Pop-Tarts.

Although, he liked Pop-Tarts, and so did she.

Maybe they should have Pop-Tarts at their wedding. That was the kind of thing couples did. Incorporate the cute foundations of their relationships into their wedding ceremonies.

She made a small sound that was halfway between a whimper and a growl. She was getting loopy about him. About a guy. Which she had promised herself she would never do. But it was hard *not* to get loopy. He had offered her support, a family for Riley, a house to live in. He had become her lover, and then he had asked to become her husband.

And in those few short moments, her entire vision for the rest of her life had changed. It had become something so much warmer, so much more secure than she had ever imagined it could be. She just wasn't strong enough to reject that vision.

Honestly, she didn't know a woman who would be strong enough. Joshua was hot. And he was nice. Well, sometimes he was kind of a jerk, but mostly, at his core, he was nice and he had wonderful taste in breakfast food.

That seemed like as good a foundation for a marriage as any.

She heard the front door open and shut, and as it slammed, her heart lurched against her breastbone.

Joshua walked in looking so intensely handsome in a light blue button-up shirt, the sleeves pushed up his arms, that she wanted to swoon for the first time in her entire life.

"Do you think they can make a wedding cake out of Pop-Tarts?" She didn't know why that was the first thing that came out of her mouth. Probably, it would have been better if she had said something about how she couldn't wait to tear his clothes off.

But no. She had led with toaster pastry.

"I don't know. But we're getting married in two weeks, so if you can stack Pop-Tarts and call them a cake, I suppose it might save time and money."

"I could probably do that. I promise that's not all I thought about today, but for some reason it's what came out of my mouth."

"How about I keep your mouth busy for a while," he said, his blue gaze getting sharp. He crossed the space between them, wrapping his arm around her waist and drawing her against him. And then he kissed her.

It was so deep, so warm, and she felt so... sheltered. Enveloped completely in his arms, in his strength. Who cared if she was lost in a fantasy right now? It would be the first time. She had never had the luxury of dreaming about men like him, or passion this intense.

It seemed right, only fair, that she have the fantasy. If only for a while. To have a moment where she actually dreamed about a wedding with cake. Where she fantasized about a man walking in the door and kissing her like this, wanting her like this.

"Is Janine here?" he asked, breaking the kiss just long enough to pose the question.

"No," she said, barely managing to answer before he slammed his lips back down on hers.

Then she found herself being lifted and carried from the entryway into the living room, deposited on the couch. And somehow, as he set her down, he managed to raise her shirt up over her head.

She stared at him, dazed, while he divested himself of his own shirt. "You're very good at this," she said. "I assume you've had a lot of practice?"

He lifted an eyebrow, his hands going to his belt buckle. "Is this a conversation you want to have?"

She felt…bemused rather than jealous. "I don't know. I'm just curious."

"I got into a lot of trouble when I was a teenager. I think I mentioned the incident with my virginity in the woods."

She nodded. "You did. And since I lost my virginity in a barn, I suppose I have to reserve judgment."

"Probably. Then I moved to Seattle. And I was even worse, because suddenly I was surrounded by women I hadn't known my whole life."

Danielle nodded gravely. "I can see how that would be an issue."

He smiled. Then finished undoing his belt, button and zipper before shoving his pants down to the floor. He stood in front of her naked, aroused and beautiful.

"Then I got myself into a long-term relationship, and it turns out I'm good at that. Well, at the being faithful part."

"That's a relief."

"In terms of promiscuity, though, my behavior has been somewhat appalling for the past five years. I have picked up a particular set of skills."

She wrinkled her nose. "I suppose that's something."

"You asked."

She straightened. "And I wanted to know."

He reached behind her back, undoing her bra, pulling it off and throwing it somewhere behind him. "Well, now you do." He pressed his hands against the back of the couch, bracketing her in. "You still want to marry me?"

"I had a very tempting proposal from the UPS man today. He asked me to sign for a package. So I guess you could say it's getting kind of serious."

"I don't think the UPS man makes you feel like this." He captured her mouth with his, and she found herself being pressed into the cushions, sliding to the side, until he'd maneuvered her so they were both lying flat on the couch.

He wrapped his fingers around her wrists, lifting them up over her head as he bent to kiss her neck, her collarbone, to draw one nipple inside his mouth.

She bucked against him, and he shifted, pushing his hand beneath her jeans, under the fabric of her panties, discovering just how wet and ready she was for him.

She rolled her hips upward, moving in time with the rhythm of his strokes, lights beginning to flash behind her eyelids, orgasm barreling down on her at an embarrassingly quick rate.

Danielle sucked in a deep breath, trying her best to hold her climax at bay. Because how embarrassing would it be to come from a kiss? A brief bit of attention to her breast and a quick stroke between the legs?

But then she opened her eyes and met his gaze. His lips curved into a wicked smile as he turned his wrist, sliding one finger deep inside her as he flicked his thumb over her clit.

All she could do then was hold on tight and ride out the explosion. He never looked away from her, and as much as she wanted to, she couldn't look away from him.

It felt too intense, too raw and much too intimate.

But she was trapped in it, drowning in it, and there was nothing she could do to stop it. She just had to surrender.

While she was still recovering from her orgasm, Joshua made quick work of her jeans, flinging them in the same direction her bra had gone.

Then, still looking right at her, he stroked her, over the thin fabric of her panties, the tease against her overly sensitized skin almost too much to handle.

Then he traced the edge of the fabric at the

crease of her thigh, dipping one finger beneath her underwear, touching slick flesh.

He hooked his finger around the fabric, pulling her panties off and casting them aside. And here she was, just as she'd been the first time, completely open and vulnerable to him. At his mercy.

It wasn't as though she didn't want that. There was something wonderful about it. Something incredible about the way he lavished attention on her, about being his sole focus.

But she wanted more. She wanted to be... She wanted to be equal to him in some way.

He was practiced. And he had skill. He'd had a lot of lovers. Realistically, she imagined he didn't even know exactly how many.

She didn't have skill. She hadn't been tutored in the art of love by anyone. But she *wanted*.

If desire could equal skill, then she could rival any woman he'd ever been with. Because the depth of her need, the depth of her passion, reached places inside her she hadn't known existed.

She pressed her hands down on the couch cushions, launching herself into a sitting position. His eyes widened, and she reveled in the fact that she had surprised him. She reached out, resting one palm against his chest, luxuriating in the feel of all that heat, that muscle, that masculine hair that tickled her sensitive skin.

"Danielle," he said, his tone filled with warning.

She didn't care about his warnings.

She was going to marry this man. He was going to be her husband. That thought filled her with such a strange sense of elation.

He had all the power. He had the money. He had the beautiful house. What he was giving her... it bordered on charity. If she was ever going to feel like she belonged—like this place was really hers—they needed to be equals in some regard.

She had to give him something too.

And if it started here, then it started here.

She leaned in, cautiously tasting his neck, tracing a line down to his nipple. He jerked beneath her touch, his reaction satisfying her in a way that went well beyond the physical.

He was beautiful, and she reveled in the chance to explore him. To run her fingertips over each well-defined muscle. Over his abs and the hard cut inward just below his hip bone.

But she didn't stop there. No, she wasn't even remotely finished with him.

He had made her shake. He had made her tremble. He had made her lose her mind.

And she was going to return the favor.

She took a deep breath and kissed his stomach. Just one easy thing before she moved on to what she wanted, even though it scared her.

She lifted her head, meeting his gaze as she wrapped her fingers around his cock and squeezed.

His eyes glittered like ice on fire, and he said nothing. He just sat there, his jaw held tight, his expression one of absolute concentration.

Then she looked away from his face, bringing her attention to that most masculine part of him. She was hungry for him. There was no other word for it.

She was starving for a taste.

And that hunger overtook everything else.

She flicked her tongue out and tasted him, his skin salty and hot. But the true eroticism was in his response. His head fell back, his breath hissing sharply through his teeth. And he reached out, pressing his hand to her back, spreading his fingers wide at the center of her shoulder blades.

Maybe she didn't have skill. Maybe she didn't know what she was doing. But he liked it. And that made her feel powerful. It made her feel needed.

She slid her hand down his shaft, gripping the base before taking him more deeply into her mouth. His groan sounded torn from him, wild and untamed, and she loved it.

Because Joshua was all about control. Had been from the moment she'd first met him.

That was what all this was, after all. From the ad in the paper to his marriage proposal—all of it was him trying to bend the situation to his will. To bend those around him to his will, to make them see he was right, that his way was the best way.

But right now he was losing control. He was at her mercy. Shaking. Because of her.

And even though she was the one pleasuring him, she felt an immense sense of satisfaction flood her as she continued to taste him. As she continued to make him tremble.

He needed her. He wanted her. After a lifetime of feeling like nobody wanted her at all, this was the most brilliant and beautiful thing she could ever imagine.

She'd heard her friends talk about giving guys blow jobs before. They laughed about it. Or said it was gross. Or said it was a great way to control their boyfriends.

They hadn't said what an incredible thing it was to make a big, strong alpha male sweat and shake. They hadn't said it could make you feel so desired, so beloved. Or that giving someone else pleasure was even better—in some ways—than being on the receiving end of the attention.

She swallowed more of him, and his hand jerked up to her hair, tugging her head back. "Careful," he said, his tone hard and thin.

"Why?"

"You keep doing that and I'm going to come," he said, not bothering to sugarcoat it.

"So what? When you did it for me, that's what I did."

"Yes. But you're a woman. And you can have

as many orgasms as I can give you without time off in between. I don't want it to end like this."

She was about to protest, but then he pulled her forward, kissing her hard and deep, stealing not just her ability to speak, but her ability to think of words.

He left her for a moment, retrieving his wallet and the protection in it, making quick work of putting the condom on before he laid her back down on the couch.

"Wait," she said, the word husky, rough. "I want… Can I be on top?"

He drew back, arching one brow. "Since you asked so nicely."

He gripped her hips, reversing their position, bringing her to sit astride him. He was hard beneath her, and she shifted back and forth experimentally, rubbing her slick folds over him before positioning him at the entrance of her body.

She bit her lip, lowering herself onto him, taking it slow, relishing that moment of him filling her so utterly and completely.

"I don't know what I'm doing," she whispered when he was buried fully inside of her.

He reached up, brushing his fingertips over her cheek before lowering his hand to grip both her hips tightly, lift her, then impale her on his hard length again.

"Just do what feels good," he ground out, the words strained.

She rocked her hips, then lifted herself slightly before taking him inside again. She repeated the motion. Again and again. Finding the speed and rhythm that made him gasp and made her moan. Finding just the right angle, just the right pressure, to please them both.

Pleasure began to ripple through her, the now somewhat familiar pressure of impending orgasm building inside her. She rolled her hips, making contact right where she needed it. He grabbed her chin, drawing her head down to kiss her. Deep, wet.

And that was it. She was done.

Pleasure burst behind her eyes, her internal muscles gripping him tight as her orgasm rocked her.

She found herself being rolled onto her back and Joshua began to pound into her, chasing his own release with a raw ferocity that made her whole body feel like it was on fire with passion.

He was undone. Completely. Because of her.

He growled, reaching beneath her to cup her ass, drawing her hard against him, forcing her to meet his every thrust. And that was when he proved himself right. She really could come as many times as he could make her.

She lost it then, shaking and shivering as her second orgasm overtook her already sensitized body.

He lowered his head, his teeth scraping against her collarbone as he froze against her, finding his own release.

He lay against her for a moment, his face buried in her neck, and she sifted her fingers through his hair, a small smile touching her lips as ripples of lingering pleasure continued to fan out through her body.

He looked at her, then brushed his lips gently over hers. She found herself being lifted up, cradled against his chest as he carried her from the couch to the stairs.

"Time for bed," he said, the words husky and rough.

She reached up and touched his face. "Okay."

He carried her to his room, laid her down on the expansive mattress, the blanket decadent and soft beneath her bare skin.

This would be their room. A room they would share.

For some reason, that thought made tears sting her eyes. She had spent so long being alone that the idea of so much closeness was almost overwhelming. But no matter what, she wanted it.

Wanted it so badly it was like a physical hunger.

Joshua joined her on the bed and she was overwhelmed by the urge to simply fold herself into his embrace. To enjoy the closeness.

But then he was naked. And so was she. So the desire for closeness fought with her desire to play with him a little more.

He pressed his hand against her lower back, then slid it down to her butt, squeezing tight. And he smiled.

Something intense and sharp filled her chest. It was almost painful.

Happiness, she realized. She was happy.

She knew in that moment that she never really had been happy before. At least, not without an equally weighty worry to balance it. To warn her that on the other side of the happiness could easily lie tragedy.

But she wasn't thinking of tragedy now. She couldn't.

Joshua filled her vision, and he filled her brain, and for now—just for now—everything in her world felt right.

For a while, she wanted that to be the whole story.

So she blocked out every other thought, every single what-if, and she kissed him again.

When Joshua woke up, the bedroom was dark. There was a woman wrapped around him. And he wasn't entirely sure what had pulled him out of his deep slumber.

Danielle was sleeping peacefully. Her dark hair was wrapped around her face like a spiderweb, and he reached down to push it back. She flinched, pursing her lips and shifting against him, tightening her arms around his waist.

She was exhausted. Probably because he was an animal who had taken her three, maybe four times before they'd finally both fallen asleep.

He looked at her, and the hunger was immediate. Visceral. And he wondered if he was fooling himself pretending, even for a moment, that any of this was for her.

That he had any kind of higher purpose.

He wondered if he had any purpose at all beyond trying to satisfy himself with her.

And then he realized what had woken him up.

He heard a high, keening cry that barely filtered through the open bedroom door. Riley.

He looked down at Danielle, who was still fast asleep, and who would no doubt be upset that they had forgotten to bring the baby monitor into the room. Joshua had barely been able to remember his own name, much less a baby monitor.

He extricated himself from her hold, scrubbing his hand over his face. Then he walked over to his closet, grabbing a pair of jeans and pulling them on with nothing underneath.

He had no idea what in the hell to do with the baby. But Danielle was exhausted, because of him, and he didn't want to wake her up.

The cries got louder as he made his way down the hall, and he walked into the room to see flailing movement coming from the crib. The baby was very unhappy, whatever the reason.

Joshua walked across the room and stood above the crib, looking down. If he was going to marry Danielle, then that meant Riley was his responsibility too.

Riley would be his son.

Something prickled at the back of his throat, making it tight. So much had happened after Shannon lost the baby that he didn't tend to think too much about what might have been. But it was impossible not to think about it right now.

His son would have been five.

He swallowed hard, trying to combat the rising tide of emotion in his chest. That emotion was why he avoided contact with Riley. Joshua wasn't so out of touch with his feelings that he didn't know that.

But his son wasn't here. He'd never had the chance to be born.

Riley was here.

And Joshua could be there for him.

He reached down, placing his hand on the baby's chest. His little body started, but he stopped crying.

Joshua didn't know the first thing about babies.

He'd never had to learn. He'd never had the chance to hold his son. Never gone through a sleepless night because of crying.

He reached down, picking up the small boy from his crib, holding the baby close to his chest and supporting Riley's downy head.

There weren't very many situations in life that caused Joshua to doubt himself. Mostly because he took great care to ensure he was only ever in situations where he had the utmost control.

But holding this tiny creature in his arms made him feel at a loss. Made him feel like his strength might be a liability rather than an asset. Because at the moment, he felt like this little boy could be far too easily broken. Like he might crush the baby somehow.

Either with his hands or with his inadequacy.

Though, he supposed that was the good thing about babies. Right now, Riley didn't seem to need him to be perfect. He just needed Joshua to be there. Being there he could handle.

He made his way to the rocking chair in the corner and sat down, pressing Riley to his chest as he rocked back and forth.

"You might be hungry," Joshua said, keeping his voice soft. "I didn't ask."

Riley turned his head back and forth, leaving a small trail of drool behind on Joshua's skin. He had a feeling if his brother could see him now, he would mock him mercilessly. But then, he couldn't imagine Isaiah with a baby at all. Devlin, yes. But only since he had married Mia. She had changed Devlin completely. Made him more relaxed. Made him a better man.

Joshua thought of Danielle, sleeping soundly back in his room. Of just how insatiable he'd been for her earlier. Of how utterly trapped she was, and more or less at his mercy.

He had to wonder if there was any way she could make him a better man, all things considered.

Though, he supposed he'd kind of started to become a better man already. Since he had taken her on. And Riley.

He had to be the man who could take care of them, if he was so intent on fixing things.

Maybe they can fix you too.

Even though there was no one in the room but the baby, Joshua shook his head. That wasn't a fair thing to put on either of them.

"Joshua?"

He looked up and saw Danielle standing in the doorway. She was wearing one of his T-shirts, the hem falling to the top of her thighs. He couldn't see her expression in the darkened room.

"Over here."

"Are you holding Riley?" She moved deeper into the room and stopped in front of him, the moonlight streaming through the window shadowing one side of her face. With her long, dark hair hanging loose around her shoulders, and that silver light casting her in a glow, she looked ethereal. He wondered how he had ever thought she was pitiful. How he had ever imagined she wasn't beautiful.

"He was crying," he responded.

"I can take him."

He shook his head, for some reason reluctant to give him up. "That's okay."

A smile curved her lips. "Okay. I can make him a bottle."

He nodded, moving his hand up and down on the baby's back. "Okay."

Danielle rummaged around for a moment and then went across the room to the changing station, where he assumed she kept the bottle-making supplies. Warmers and filtered water and all of that. He didn't know much about it, only that he had arranged to have it all delivered to the house to make things easier for her.

She returned a moment later, bottle in hand. She tilted it upside down and tested it on the inside of her wrist. "It's all good. Do you want to give it to him?"

He nodded slowly and reached up. "Sure."

He shifted his hold on Riley, repositioning him in the crook of his arm so he could offer him the bottle.

"Do you have a lot of experience with babies?"

"None," he said.

"You could have fooled me. Although, I didn't really have any experience with babies until Riley was born. I didn't figure I would ever have experience with them."

"No?"

She shook her head. "No. I was never going to get married, Joshua. I knew all about men, you see. My mother got pregnant with me when she was fourteen. Needless to say, things didn't get off to the best start. I never knew my father. My upbringing was…unstable. My mother just wasn't ready to have a baby, and honestly, I don't know how she could have been. She didn't have a good home life, and she was so young. I think she wanted to keep me, wanted to do the right thing—it was just hard. She was always looking for something else. Looking for love."

"Not in the right places, I assume."

She bit her lip. "No. To say the least. She had a lot of boyfriends, and we lived with some of them. Sometimes that was better. Sometimes they were more established than us and had better homes. The older I got, the less like a mom my mom seemed. I started to really understand how young she was. When she would get her heart broken, I comforted her more like a friend than like a daughter. When she would go out and get drunk, I would put her to bed like I was the parent." Danielle took a deep breath. "I just didn't want that for myself. I didn't want to depend on anybody, or have anyone depend on me. I didn't want to pin my hopes on someone else. And I never saw a relationship that looked like anything else when I was growing up."

"But here you are," he said, his chest feeling tight. "And you're marrying me."

"I don't know if you can possibly understand what this is like," she said, laughing, a kind of shaky nervous sound. "Having this idea of what your life will be and just…changing that. I was so certain about what I would have, and what I wouldn't have. I would never get married. I would never have children. I would never have…a beautiful house or a yard." Her words got thick, her throat sounding tight. "Then there was Riley. And then there was your ad. And then there was you. And suddenly everything I want is different, everything I expect is different. I actually hope for things. It's kind of a miracle."

He wanted to tell her that he wasn't a miracle. That whatever she expected from him, he was sure to disappoint her in some way. But what she was describing was too close to his own truth.

He had written off having a wife. He had written off having children. That was the whole part of being human he'd decided wasn't for him. And yet here he was, feeding a baby at three in the morning staring at a woman who had just come from his bed. A woman who was wearing his ring.

The way Joshua needed it, the way he wanted to cling to his new reality, to make sure that it was real and that it would last, shocked him with its ferocity.

A moment later, he heard a strange sucking sound and realized the bottle was empty.

"Am I supposed to burp him?"

Danielle laughed. "Yes. But I'll do that."

"I'm not helpless."

"He's probably going to spit up on your hot and sexy chest. Better to have him do it on your T-shirt." She reached out. "I got this."

She took Riley from him and he sat back and admired the expert way she handled the little boy. She rocked him over her shoulder, patting his back lightly until he made a sound that most definitely suggested he had spit up on the T-shirt she was wearing.

Joshua had found her to be such a strange creature when he had first seen her. Brittle and pointed. Fragile.

But she was made of iron. He could see that now.

No one had been there to raise her, not really. And then she had stepped in to make sure that her half brother was taken care of. Had upended every plan she'd made for her life and decided to become a mother at twenty-two.

"What?" she asked, and he realized he had been sitting there staring at her.

"You're an amazing woman, Danielle Kelly. And if no one's ever told you that, it's about time someone did."

She was so bright, so beautiful, so fearless.

All this time she had been a burning flame no one had taken the time to look at. But she had come to him, answered his ad and started a wildfire in his life.

It didn't seem fair, the way the world saw each of them. He was a celebrated businessman, and she... Well, hadn't he chosen her because he knew his family would simply see her as a poor, unwed mother?

She was worth ten of him.

She blinked rapidly and wasn't quite able to stop a tear from tracking down her cheek. "Why...why do you think that?"

"Not very many people would have done what you did. Taking your brother. Not after everything your mother already put you through. Not after spending your whole life taking care of the one person who should have been taking care of you. And then you came here and answered my ad."

"Some people might argue that the last part was taking the easy way out."

"Right. Except that I could have been a serial killer."

"Or made me dress like a teddy bear," she said,

keeping her tone completely serious. "I actually feel like that last one is more likely."

"Do you?"

"There are more furries than there are serial killers, thank God."

"I guess, lucky for you, I'm neither one." He wasn't sure he was the great hope she seemed to think he was. But right now, he wanted to be.

"Very lucky for me," she said. "Oh…Joshua, imagine if someone were both."

"I'd rather not."

She went to the changing table and quickly set about getting Riley a new diaper before placing him back in the crib. Then she straightened and hesitated. "I guess I could… I can just stay in here. Or…"

"Get the baby monitor," he said. "You're coming back to my bed."

She smiled, and she did just that.

The next day there were wedding dresses in Danielle's room. Not just a couple of wedding dresses. At least ten, all in her size.

She turned in a circle, looking at all of the garment bags with heavy white satin, beads and chiffon showing through.

Joshua walked into the room behind her, his arms folded over his chest. She raised her eyebrows, gesturing wildly at the dresses. "What is this?"

"We are getting married in less than two weeks. You need a dress."

"A fancy dress to eat my Pop-Tart cake in," she said, moving to a joke because if she didn't she might cry. Because the man had ordered wedding dresses and brought them into the house.

And because if she were normal, she might have friends to share this occasion with her. Or her mother. Instead, she was standing in her bedroom, where her baby was napping, and her fiancé was the only potential spectator.

"You aren't supposed to see the dresses, though," she said.

"I promise you I cannot make any sense out of them based on how they look stuffed into those bags. I called the bridal store in town and described your figure and had her send dresses accordingly."

Her eyes flew wide, her mouth dropping open. "You described my figure?"

"To give her an idea of what would suit you."

"I'm going to need a play-by-play of this description. How did you describe my figure, Joshua? This is very important."

"Elfin," he said, surprising her because he didn't seem to be joking. And that was a downright fanciful description coming from him.

"Elfin?"

A smile tipped his lips upward. "Yes. You're like an elf. Or a nymph."

"Nympho, maybe. And I blame you for that."

He reached out then, hooking his arm around her waist and drawing her toward him. "Danielle, I am serious."

She swallowed hard. "Okay," she said, because she didn't really know what else to say.

"You're beautiful."

Hearing him say that made her throat feel all dry and scratchy, made her eyes feel like they were burning. "You don't have to do that," she said.

"You think I'm lying? Why would I lie about that? Also, men can't fake this." He grabbed her hand and pressed it up against the front of his jeans, against the hardness there.

"You're asking me to believe your penis? Because penises are notoriously indiscriminate."

"You have a point. Plus, mine is pretty damn famously indiscriminate. By my own admission. But the one good thing about that is you can trust I know the difference between generalized lust and when a woman has reached down inside of me and grabbed hold of something I didn't even know was there. I told you, I like it easy. I told you…I don't deal with difficult situations or difficult people. That was my past failing. A huge failing, and I don't know if I'm ever going to forgive myself for it. But what we have here makes me feel like maybe I can make up for it."

There were a lot of nice words in there. A lot of

beautiful sentiments tangled up in something that made her feel, well, kind of gross.

But he was looking at her with all that intensity, and there were wedding dresses hung up all around her, his ring glittering on her finger. And she just didn't want to examine the bad feelings. She was so tired of bad feelings.

Joshua—all of this—was like a fantasy. She wanted to live in the fantasy for as long as she could.

Was that wrong? After everything she had been through, she couldn't believe that it was.

"Well, get your penis out of here. The rest of you too. I'm going to try on dresses."

"I don't get to watch?"

"I grant you nothing about our relationship has been typical so far, but I would like to surprise you with my dress choice."

"That's fair. Why don't you let me take Riley for a while?"

"Janine is going to be here soon."

He shrugged. "I'll take him until then." He strode across the room and picked Riley up, and Riley flashed a small, gummy smile that might have been nothing more than a facial twitch but still made Danielle's heart do something fluttery and funny.

Joshua's confidence with Riley was increasing,

and he made a massive effort to be proactive when it came to taking care of the baby.

Watching Joshua stand there with Riley banished any lingering gross feelings about being considered difficult, and when Joshua left the room and Danielle turned to face the array of gowns, she pushed every last one of her doubts to the side.

Maybe Joshua wasn't perfect. Maybe there were some issues. But all of this, with him, was a damn sight better than anything she'd had before.

And a girl like her couldn't afford to be too picky.

She took a deep breath and unzipped the first dress.

Ten

The day of the wedding was drawing closer and Danielle was drawing closer to a potential nervous breakdown. She was happy, in a way. When Joshua kissed her, when he took her to bed, when he spent the whole night holding her in his strong arms, everything felt great.

It was the in-between hours. The quiet moments she spent with herself, rocking Riley in that gray time before dawn. That was when she pulled those bad feelings out and began to examine them.

She had two days until the wedding, and her dress had been professionally altered to fit her—a glorious, heavy satin gown with a deep V in the

back and buttons that ran down the full skirt—
and if for no other reason than that, she couldn't
back out.

The thought of backing out sent a burst of pain
blooming through her chest. Unfurling, spreading,
expanding. No. She didn't want to leave Joshua. No
matter the strange, imbalanced feelings between
them, she wanted to be with him. She felt almost
desperate to be with him.

She looked over at him now, sitting in the
driver's seat of what was still the nicest car she
had ever touched, much less ridden in, as they
pulled up to the front of his parents' house.

Sometimes looking at him hurt. And sometimes
looking away from him hurt. Sometimes everything hurt. The need to be near him, the need for
distance.

Maybe she really had lost her mind.

It took her a moment to realize she was still sitting motionless in the passenger seat, and Joshua
had already put the car in Park and retrieved Riley
from the back seat. He didn't bother to bring the
car seat inside this time. Instead, he wrapped the
baby in a blanket and cradled him in his arms.

Oh, that hurt her in a whole different way.

Joshua was sexy. All the time. There was no
question about that. But the way he was with
Riley... Well, she was surprised that any woman

who walked by him when he was holding Riley didn't fall immediately at his feet.

She nearly did. Every damned time.

She followed him to the front door, looking down to focus on the way the gravel crunched beneath her boots—new boots courtesy of Joshua that didn't have holes in them, and didn't need three pairs of socks to keep her toes from turning into icicles—because otherwise she was going to get swallowed up by the nerves that were riding through her.

His mother had insisted on making a prewedding dinner for them, and this was Danielle's second chance to make a first impression. Now it was real and she felt an immense amount of pressure to be better than she was, rather than simply sliding into the lowest expectation people like his family had of someone like her, as she'd done before.

She looked over at him when she realized he was staring at her. "You're going to be fine," he said.

Then he bent down and kissed her. She closed her eyes, her breath rushing from her lungs as she gave herself over to his kiss.

That, of course, was when the front door opened.

"You're here!"

Nancy Grayson actually looked happy to see them both, and even happier that she had caught them making out on the front porch.

Danielle tucked a stray lock of hair behind her ear. "Thank you for doing this," she said, jarred by the change in her role, but desperate to do a good job.

"Of course," the older woman said. "Now, let me hold my grandbaby."

Those words made Danielle pause, made her freeze up. Made her want to cry. Actually, she *was* crying. Tears were rolling down her cheeks without even giving her a chance to hold them back.

Joshua's mother frowned. "What's wrong, honey?"

Danielle swallowed hard. "I didn't ever expect that he would have grandparents. That he would have a family." She took a deep breath. "I mean like this. It means a lot to me."

Nancy took Riley from Joshua's arms. But then she reached out and put her hand on Danielle's shoulder. "He's not the only one who has a family. You do too."

Throughout the evening Danielle was stunned by the warm acceptance of Joshua's entire family. By the way his sister-in-law, Mia, made an effort to get to know her, and by the complete absence of antagonism coming from his younger sister, Faith.

But what really surprised her was when Joshua's father came and sat next to her on the couch during dessert. Joshua was engaged in conversation with his brothers across the room while Mia, Faith and Joshua's mother were busy playing with Riley.

"I knew you would be good for him," Mr. Grayson said.

Danielle looked up at the older man. "A wife, you mean," she said, her voice soft. She didn't know why she had challenged his assertion, why she'd done anything but blandly agree. Except she knew she wasn't the woman he would have chosen for his son, and she didn't want him to pretend otherwise.

He shook his head. "I'm not talking about the ad. I know what he did. I know that he placed another ad looking for somebody he could use to get back at me. But the minute I met you, I knew you were exactly what he needed. Somebody unexpected. Somebody who would push him out of his comfort zone. It's real now, isn't it?"

It's real now.

Those words echoed inside of her. What did real mean? They were really getting married, but was their relationship real?

He didn't love her. He wanted to fix her. And somehow, through fixing her, he believed he would fix himself.

Maybe that wasn't any less real than what most people had. Maybe it was just more honest.

"Yes," she said, her voice a whisper. "It's real."

"I know that my meddling upset him. I'm not

stupid. And I know he felt like I wasn't listening to him. But he has been so lost in all that pain, and I knew… I knew he just needed to love somebody again. He thought everything I did, everything I said was because I don't understand a life that goes beyond what we have here." He gestured around the living room—small, cozy, essentially a stereotype of the happy, rural family. "But that's not it. Doesn't matter what a life looks like, a man needs love. And *that* man needs love more than most. He always was stubborn, difficult. Never could get him to talk about much of anything. He needs someone he can talk to. Someone who can see the good in him so he can start to see it too."

"Love," Danielle said softly, the word a revelation she had been trying to avoid.

That was why it hurt. When she looked at him. When she was with him. When she looked away from him. When he was gone.

That was the intense, building pressure inside her that felt almost too large for her body to contain.

It was every beautiful, hopeful feeling she'd had since meeting him.

She loved him.

And he didn't love her. That absence was the cause of the dark disquiet she'd felt sometimes. He wanted to use her as a substitute for his girlfriend, the one he thought he had failed.

"Every man needs love," Todd said. "Successful businessmen and humble farmers. Trust me. It's the thing that makes life run. The thing that keeps you going when crops don't grow and the weather doesn't cooperate. The thing that pulls you up from the dark pit when you can't find the light. I'm glad he found his light."

But he hadn't.

She had found hers.

For him, she was a Band-Aid he was trying to put over a wound that would end up being fatal if he didn't do something to treat it. If he didn't do something more than simply cover it up.

She took a deep breath. "I don't…"

"Are you ready to go home?"

Danielle looked up and saw Joshua standing in front of her. And those words…

Him asking if she wanted to go home, meaning to his house, with him, like that house belonged to her. Like he belonged to her…

Well, his question allowed her to erase all the doubts that had just washed through her. Allowed her to put herself back in the fantasy she'd been living in since she'd agreed to his proposal.

"Sure," she said, pushing herself up from the couch.

She watched as he said goodbye to his family, as he collected Riley and slung the diaper bag over his shoulder. Yes. She loved him.

She was an absolute and total lost cause for him. In love. Something she had thought she could never be.

The only problem was, she was in love alone.

It was his wedding day.

Thankfully, only his family would be in attendance. A small wedding in Copper Ridge's Baptist church, which was already decorated for Christmas and so saved everyone time and hassle.

Which was a good thing, since he had already harassed local baker Alison Donnelly to the point where she was ready to assault him with a spatula over his demands related to a Pop-Tart cake.

It was the one thing Danielle had said she wanted, and even if she had been joking, he wanted to make it happen for her.

He liked doing things for her. Whether it was teaching her how to ride horses, pleasuring her in the bedroom or fixing her nice meals, she always expressed a deep and sweet gratitude that transcended anything he had ever experienced before.

Her appreciation affected him. He couldn't pretend it didn't.

She affected him.

He walked into the empty church, looking up at the steeply pitched roof and the thick, curved beams of wood that ran the length of it, currently decked with actual boughs of holly.

Everything looked like it was set up and ready, all there was to do now was wait for the ceremony to start.

Suddenly, the doors that led to the fellowship hall opened wide and in burst Danielle. If he had thought she looked ethereal before, it was nothing compared to how she looked at this moment. Her dark hair was swept back in a loose bun, sprigs of baby's breath woven into it, some tendrils hanging around her face.

And the dress...

The bodice was fitted, showing off her slim figure, and the skirt billowed out around her, shimmering with each and every step. She was holding a bouquet of dark red roses, her lips painted a deep crimson to match.

"I didn't think I was supposed to see you until the wedding?" It was a stupid thing to say, but it was about the only thing he could think of.

"Yes. I know. I was here getting ready, and I was going to hide until everything started. Stay in the dressing room." She shook her head. "I need to talk to you, though. And I was already wearing this dress, and all of the layers of underwear that you have to wear underneath it to make it do this." She kicked her foot out, causing the skirt to flare.

"To make it do what?"

"You need a crinoline. Otherwise your skirt is like a wilted tulip. That's something I learned when the wedding store lady came this morning to help me get ready. But that's not what I wanted to talk to you about."

He wasn't sure if her clarification was a relief or not. He wasn't an expert on the subject of crinolines, but it seemed like an innocuous subject. Anything else that had drawn her out of hiding before the ceremony probably wasn't.

"Then talk."

She took a deep breath, wringing her hands around the stem of her bouquet. "Okay. I will talk. I'm going to. In just a second."

He shook his head. "Danielle Kelly, you stormed into my house with a baby and pretty much refused to leave until I agreed to give you what you wanted—don't act like you're afraid of me now."

"That was different. I wasn't afraid of losing you then." She looked up at him, her dark eyes liquid. "I'm afraid right now."

"You?" He couldn't imagine this brave, wonderfully strong woman being afraid of anything.

"I've never had anything that I wanted to keep. Or I guess, I never did before Riley. Once I had him, the thought of losing him was one of the things that scared me. It was the first time I'd ever felt anything like it. And now…it's the same with you. Do you know what you have in common with Riley?"

"The occasional tantrum?" His chest was tight.

He knew that was the wrong thing to say, knew it was wrong to make light of the situation when she was so obviously serious and trembling.

"Fair enough," she said. Then she took a deep breath. "I love you. That's what you have in common with Riley. That's why I'm afraid of losing you. Because you matter. Because you more than matter. You're…everything."

Her words were like a sucker punch straight to the gut. "Danielle…"

He was such an ass. Of course she thought she was in love with him. He was her first lover, the first man to ever give her an orgasm. He had offered her a place to live and he was promising a certain amount of financial security, the kind she'd never had before.

Of course such a vulnerable, lonely woman would confuse those feelings of gratitude with love.

She frowned. "Don't use that tone with me. I know you're about to act like you're the older and wiser of the two of us. You're about to explain why I don't understand what I'm talking about. Remember when you told me about your penis?"

He looked over his shoulder, then back at Danielle. "Okay, I'm not usually a prude, but we are in a church."

She let out an exasperated sound. "Sorry. But the thing is, remember when you told me that because you had been indiscriminate you knew the difference between common, garden-variety sex—"

"Danielle, Pastor John is around here somewhere."

She straightened her arms at her sides, the flowers in her hand trembling with her unsuppressed irritation. "Who cares? This is our life. Anyway, what little I've read in the Bible was pretty honest about people. Everything I'm talking about—it's all part of being a person. I'm not embarrassed about any of it." She tilted her chin up, looking defiant. "My point is, I don't need you telling me what you think I feel. I have spent so much time alone, so much time without love, that I've had a lot of time to think about what it might feel like. About what it might mean."

He lowered his voice and took a step toward her. "Danielle, feeling cared for isn't the same as love. Pleasure isn't the same as love."

"I know that!" Her words echoed in the empty sanctuary. "Trust me. If I thought being taken care of was the same thing as love, I probably would have repeated my mother's pattern for my entire life. But I didn't. I waited. I waited until I found a man who was worth being an idiot over. Here I am in a wedding dress yelling at the man I'm supposed to marry in an hour, wanting him to understand that I love him. You can't be much more of an idiot than that, Joshua."

"It's okay if you love me," he said, even though it made his stomach feel tight. Even though it wasn't okay at all. "But I don't know what you expect me to do with that."

She stamped her foot, the sound ricocheting around them. "Love me back, dammit."

He felt like someone had grabbed hold of his heart and squeezed it hard. "Danielle, I can't do that. I can't. And honestly, it's better if you don't feel that way about me. I think we can have a partnership. I'm good with those. I'm good with making agreements, shaking hands, holding up my end of the deal. But feelings, all that stuff in between… I would tell you to call Shannon and ask her about that, but I don't think she has a phone right now, because I'm pretty sure she's homeless."

"You can't take the blame for that. You can't take the blame for her mistakes. I mean, I guess you can, you've been doing a great job of it for the past five years. And I get that. You lost a child. And then you lost your fiancée, the woman you loved. And you're holding on to that pain to try to insulate yourself from more."

He shook his head. "That's not it. It would be damned irresponsible of me not to pay attention to what I did to her. To what being with me can do to a woman." He cleared his throat. "She needed something that I couldn't give. I did love her—you're right. But it wasn't enough."

"You're wrong about that too," she said. "You loved her enough. But sometimes, Joshua, you can love somebody and love somebody, but unless they do something with that love it goes fallow. You can sow the seeds all you want, but if they don't water them, if they don't nurture them, you can't fix it for them."

"I didn't do enough," he said, tightening his jaw, hardening his heart.

"Maybe you were difficult. Maybe you did some wrong things. But at some point, she needed to reach out and tell you that. But she didn't. She shut down. Love can be everything, but it can't all be coming from one direction. The other person has to accept it. You can't love someone into being whole. They have to love themselves enough to want to be whole. And they have to love you enough to lay down their pain, to lay down their selfishness, and change—even when it's hard."

"I can't say she was selfish," he said, his voice rough. "I can't say she did anything wrong."

"What about my mother? God knows she had it hard, Joshua. I can't imagine having a baby at fourteen. It's hard enough having one at twenty-two. She has a lot of excuses. And they're valid. She went through hell, but the fact of the matter is she's choosing to go through it at this point. She has spent her whole life searching for the kind of love that either one of her children would have given her for nothing. I couldn't have loved her more. Riley is a baby, completely and totally dependent on whoever might take care of him. Could we have loved her more? Could we have made her stay?"

"That's different."

She stamped her foot again. "It is fucking not!"

He didn't bother to yell at her about them being in a church again. "I understand that all of this is new to you," he said, fighting to keep his voice steady. "And honestly? It feels good, selfishly good, to know you see all this in me. It's tempting to lie to you, Danielle. But I can't do that. What I offered you is the beginning and end of what I have. Either you accept our partnership or you walk away."

She wouldn't.

She needed him too much. That was the part that made him a monster.

He knew he had all the power here, and he knew she would ultimately see things his way. She would have to.

And then what? Would she wither away living with him? Wanting something that he refused to give her?

The situation looked too familiar.

He tightened his jaw, steeling himself for her response.

What he didn't expect was to find a bouquet of flowers tossed at him. He caught them, and her petite shoulders lifted up, then lowered as she let out a shuddering breath. "I guess you're the next one to get married, then. Congratulations. You caught the flowers."

"Of course I damn well am," he said, tightening his fist around the roses, ignoring the thorn that bit into his palm. "Our wedding is in an hour."

Her eyes filled with tears, and she shook her head. Then she turned and ran out of the room, pausing only to kick her shoes off and leave them lying on the floor like she was Cinderella.

And he just stood there, holding on to the flowers, a trickle of blood from the thorn dripping down his wrist as he watched the first ray of light, the first bit of hope he'd had in years, disappear from his life.

Of course, her exit didn't stop him from standing at the altar and waiting. Didn't stop him from acting like the wedding would continue without a hitch.

He knew she hadn't gone far, mostly because Janine was still at the church with Riley, and while Danielle's actions were painful and mystifying at the moment, he knew her well enough to know she wasn't going to leave without Riley.

But the music began to play and no bride materialized.

There he was, a giant dick in a suit, waiting for a woman who wasn't going to come.

His family looked at each other, trading expressions filled with a mix of pity and anger. But it was his father who spoke up. "What in hell did you do, boy?"

A damned good question.

Unfortunately, he knew the answer to it.

"Why are you blaming him?" Faith asked, his younger sister defending him to the bitter end, even when he didn't deserve it.

"Because that girl loves him," his father said, his tone full of confidence, "and she wouldn't have left him standing there if he hadn't done something."

Pastor John raised his hands, the gesture clearly meant to placate. "If there are any doubts about a marriage, it's definitely best to stop and consider those doubts, as it is a union meant for life."

"And she was certain," Joshua's father said. "Which means he messed it up."

"When two people love each other..." The rest of Pastor John's words were swallowed up by Joshua's family, but those first six hit Joshua and pierced him right in the chest.

When two people love each other.

Two people. Loving each other.

Love going both ways. Giving and taking.

And he understood then. He really understood.

Why she couldn't submit to living in a relationship that she thought might be one-sided. Because she had already endured it once. Because she'd already lived it with her mother.

Danielle was willing to walk away from everything he'd offered her. From the house, from the money, from the security. Even from his family. Because for some reason his love meant that much to her.

That realization nearly brought him to his knees.

He had thought his love insufficient. Had thought it destructive. And as she had stood there, pleading with him to love her back, he had thought his love unimportant.

But to her, it was everything.

How dare he question her feelings for him? Love, to Danielle, was more than a ranch and good sex. And she had proved it, because she was clearly willing to sacrifice the ranch and the sex to have him return her love.

"It was my fault," he said, his voice sounding like a stranger's as it echoed through the room. "She said she loved me. And I told her I couldn't love her back."

"Well," Faith said, "not even I can defend you now, dumbass."

His mother looked stricken, his father angry. His brothers seemed completely unsurprised.

"You do love her, though," his father said, his tone steady. "So why did you tell her you didn't?"

Of course, Joshua realized right then something else she'd been right about. He was afraid.

Afraid of wanting this life he really had always dreamed of but had written off because he messed up his first attempt so badly. Afraid because the first time had been so painful, had gone so horribly wrong.

"Because I'm a coward," he said. "But I'm not going to be one anymore."

He walked down off the stage and to the front pew, picking up the bouquet. "I'm going to go find her," he said. "I know she's not far, since Riley is here."

Suddenly, he knew exactly where she was.

"Do you have any other weddings today, Pastor?"

Pastor John shook his head. "No. This is the only thing I have on my schedule today. Not many people get married on a Thursday."

"Hopefully, if I don't mess this up, we'll need you."

Eleven

It was cold. And Danielle's bare feet were starting to ache. But there had been no way in hell she could run in those high heels. She would have broken her neck.

Of course, if she had broken her neck, she might have fully severed her spinal cord and then not been able to feel anything. A broken heart sadly didn't work that way. She felt everything. Pain, deep and unending. Pain that spread from her chest out to the tips of her fingers and toes.

She wiggled her toes. In fairness, they might just be frostbitten.

She knew she was being pathetic. Lying down

on that Pendleton blanket in the loft. The place where Joshua had first made love to her. Hiding.

Facing everyone—facing Joshua again—was inevitable. She was going to have to get Riley. Pack up her things.

Figure out life without Joshua's money. Go back to working a cash register at a grocery store somewhere. Wrestling with childcare problems.

She expected terror to clutch her at the thought. Expected to feel deep sadness about her impending poverty. But those feelings didn't come.

She really didn't care about any of that.

Well, she probably would care once she was neck deep in it again, but right now all she cared about was that she wouldn't have Joshua.

If he had no money, if he was struggling just like her, she would have wanted to struggle right along with him.

But money or no money, struggle or no struggle, she needed him to love her. Otherwise...

She closed her eyes and took in a breath of sharp, cold air.

She had been bound and determined to ignore all of the little warnings she'd felt in her soul when she'd thought about their relationship. But in the end, she couldn't.

She knew far too well what it was like to pour love out and never get it back. And for a while it had been easy to pretend. That his support, and the sex, was the same as getting something back.

But they were temporary.

The kinds of things that would fade over the years.

If none of his choices were rooted in love, if none of it was founded in love, then what they had couldn't last.

She was saving herself hideous heartbreak down the road by stabbing herself in the chest now.

She snorted. Right now, she kind of wondered what the point was.

Pride?

"Screw pride," she croaked.

She heard the barn door open, heard footsteps down below, and she curled up into a ball, the crinoline under her dress scratching her legs. She buried her face in her arm, like a child. As if whoever had just walked into the barn wouldn't be able to see her as long as she couldn't see him.

Then she heard footsteps on the ladder rungs, the sound of calloused hands sliding over the metal. She knew who it was. Oh well. She had already embarrassed herself in front of him earlier. It was not like him seeing her sprawled in a tragic heap in a barn was any worse than her stamping her foot like a dramatic silent-film heroine.

"I thought I might find you here."

She didn't look up when she heard his voice.

Instead, she curled into a tighter, even more reso-
lute ball.

She felt him getting closer, which was ridiculous. She knew she couldn't actually feel the heat
radiating from his body.

"I got you that Pop-Tart cake," he said. "I mean,
I had Alison from Pie in the Sky make one. And
I have to tell you, it looks disgusting. I mean, she
did a great job, but I can't imagine that it's edible."

She uncurled as a sudden spout of rage flooded
through her and she pushed herself into a sitting
position. "Fuck your Pop-Tart cake, Joshua."

"I thought we both liked Pop-Tarts."

"Yes. But I don't like lies. And your Pop-Tarts
would taste like lies."

"Actually," he said slowly, "I think the Pop-Tart
cake is closer to the truth than anything I said to
you back in the church. You said a lot of things
that were true. I'm a coward, Danielle. And guilt
is a hell of a lot easier than grief."

"What the hell does that mean?" She drew her
arm underneath her nose, wiping snot and tears
away, tempted to ask him where his elfin princess
was now. "Don't tease me. Don't talk in riddles.
I'm ready to walk away from you if I need to, but
I don't want to do it. So please, don't tempt me to
hurt myself like that if you aren't…"

"I love you," he said, his voice rough. "And
my saying so now isn't because I was afraid you

were a gold digger and you proved you weren't by walking away. I realize what I'm about to say could be confused for that, but don't be confused. Because loving you has nothing to do with that. If you need my money... I've never blamed you for going after it. I've never blamed you for wanting to make your and Riley's lives easier. But the fact that you *were* willing to walk away from everything over three words... How can I pretend they aren't important? How can I pretend that I don't need your love when you demonstrated that you need my love more than financial security. More than sex. How can I doubt you and the strength of your feelings? How can I excuse my unwillingness to open myself up to you? My unwillingness to make myself bleed for you?"

He reached out, taking hold of her hands, down on his knees with her.

"You're going to get your suit dirty," she said inanely.

"Your dress is filthy," he returned.

She looked down at the dirt and smudges on the beautiful white satin. "Crap."

He took hold of her chin, tilting her face up to look at him. "I don't care. It doesn't matter. Because I would marry you in blue jeans, or I would marry you in this barn. I would sure as hell marry you in that dirty wedding dress. I... You are right about everything.

"It was easy to martyr myself over Shannon's pain. To blame myself so I didn't have to try again. So I didn't have to hurt again. Old pain is easier. The pain from that time in my life isn't gone, but it's dull. It throbs sometimes. It aches. When I look at Riley, he reminds me of my son, who never took a breath, and it hurts down deep. But I know that if I were to lose either of you now… That would be fresh pain. A fresh hell. And I have some idea of what that hell would be like because of what I've been through before.

"But it would be worse now. And…I was protecting myself from it. But now, I don't care about the pain, the fear. I want it all. I want you.

"I love you. Whatever might happen, whatever might come our way in the future… I love you. And I am going to do the hard fucking yards for you, Danielle."

His expression was so fierce, his words so raw and real, all she could do was stare at him, listening as he said all the things she had never imagined she would hear.

"I was young and stupid the last time I tried love. Selfish. I made mistakes. I can't take credit for everything that went wrong. Some of it was fate. Some of it was her choices. But when things get hard this time, you have my word I won't pull away. I'm not going to let you shut me out. If you close the door on me, I'm going to kick it down.

Because what we have is special. It's real. It's hope. And I will fight with everything I have to hold on to it."

She lurched forward, wrapping her arms around his neck, making them both fall backward. "I'll never shut you out." She squeezed her eyes closed, tears tracking down her cheeks. "Finding you has been the best thing that's ever happened to me. I don't feel alone, Joshua. Can you possibly understand what that means to me?"

He nodded gravely, kissing her lips. "I do understand," he said. "Because I've been alone in my own swamp for a long damned time. And you're the first person who made me feel like it was worth it to wade out."

"I love you," she said.

"I love you too. Do you still want to marry me?"

"Hell yeah."

"Good." He maneuvered them both so they were upright, taking her hand and leading her to the ladder. They climbed down, and she hopped from foot to foot on the cold cement floor. "Come on," he said, grabbing her hand and leading her through the open double doors.

She stopped when she saw that his whole family, Janine and Riley, and Pastor John were standing out there in the gravel.

Joshua's mother was holding the bouquet of roses, and she reached out, handing it back to

Danielle. Then Joshua went to Janine and took Riley from her arms, holding the baby in the crook of his own. Then Joshua went back to Danielle, taking both of her hands with his free one.

"I look bedraggled," she said.

"You look perfect to me."

She smiled, gazing at everyone, at her new family. At this new life she was going to have.

And then she looked back at the man she loved with all her heart. "Well," she said, "okay, then. Marry me, cowboy."

Epilogue

December 5, 2017
FOUND A WIFE—

Local rancher Todd Grayson and his wife, Nancy, are pleased to announce the marriage of their son, a wealthy former bachelor, Joshua Grayson (no longer irritated with his father) to Danielle Kelly, formerly of Portland, now of Copper Ridge and the daughter of their hearts. Mr. Grayson knew his son would need a partner who was strong, determined and able to handle an extremely stubborn cuss, which she does beautifully.

But best of all, she loves him with her whole heart, which is all his meddling parents ever wanted for him.

* * * * *

Meet all the cowboys in Copper Ridge!

"SHOULDA BEEN A COWBOY"
PART TIME COWBOY
BROKEDOWN COWBOY
BAD NEWS COWBOY
"A COPPER RIDGE CHRISTMAS"
"HOMETOWN HEARTBREAKER"
ONE NIGHT CHARMER
TAKE ME, COWBOY
TOUGH LUCK HERO
LAST CHANCE REBEL
HOLD ME, COWBOY
SEDUCE ME, COWBOY

* * *

If you're on Twitter,
tell us what you think of Harlequin Desire!
#harlequindesire

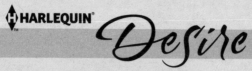
#2587 AN HONORABLE SEDUCTION
The Westmoreland Legacy • by Brenda Jackson
Navy SEAL David "Flipper" Holloway has one mission: get close to gorgeous store owner Swan Jamison and find out all he can. But flirtation leads to seduction and he's about to get caught between duty and the woman he vows to claim as his...

#2588 REUNITED...WITH BABY
Texas Cattleman's Club: The Impostor • by Sara Orwig
Wealthy tech tycoon Luke has come home and he'll do whatever it takes to revive his family's ranch. Even hire the woman he left behind, veterinarian and single mother Scarlett. He can't say yes to forever, but will one more night be enough?

#2589 THE TWIN BIRTHRIGHT
Alaskan Oil Barons • by Catherine Mann
When reclusive inventor Royce Miller is reunited with his ex-fiancée and her twin babies in a snowstorm, he vows to protect them at all costs—even if the explosive chemistry that drove them apart is stronger than ever!

#2590 THE ILLEGITIMATE BILLIONAIRE
Billionaires and Babies • by Barbara Dunlop
Black sheep Deacon Holt, illegitimate son of a billionaire, must marry the gold-digging widow of his half brother if he wants his family's recognition. Actually desiring the beautiful single mother isn't part of the plan, especially when she has shocking relevations of her own...

#2591 WRONG BROTHER, RIGHT MAN
Switching Places • by Kat Cantrell
To inherit his fortune, flirtatious Valentino LeBlanc must swap roles with his too-serious brother. He'll prove he's just as good as, if not better than, his brother. At everything. But when he hires his brother's ex to advise him, things won't stay professional for long...

#2592 ONE NIGHT TO FOREVER
The Ballantyne Billionaires • by Joss Wood
When Lachlyn is outed as a long-lost Ballantyne heiress, wealthy security expert Reame vows to protect her. She's his best friend's sister, an innocent... Surely he can keep his hands to himself. But all it takes is one night to ignite a passion that could burn them both...

Get 2 Free Books,
Plus 2 Free Gifts—
just for trying the Reader Service!

YES! Please send me 2 FREE Harlequin® Desire novels and my 2 FREE gifts (gifts are worth about $10 retail). After receiving them, if I don't wish to receive any more books, I can return the shipping statement marked "cancel." If I don't cancel, I will receive 6 brand-new novels every month and be billed just $4.55 per book in the U.S. or $5.24 per book in Canada. That's a savings of at least 13% off the cover price! It's quite a bargain! Shipping and handling is just 50¢ per book in the U.S. and 75¢ per book in Canada*. I understand that accepting the 2 free books and gifts places me under no obligation to buy anything. I can always return a shipment and cancel at any time. The free books and gifts are mine to keep no matter what I decide.

225/326 HDN GMWG

Name _____ (PLEASE PRINT)

Address _____ Apt. #

City _____ State/Prov. _____ Zip/Postal Code

Signature (if under 18, a parent or guardian must sign)

Mail to the **Reader Service:**
IN U.S.A.: P.O. Box 1341, Buffalo, NY 14240-8531
IN CANADA: P.O. Box 603, Fort Erie, Ontario L2A 5X3

Want to try two free books from another line?
Call 1-800-873-8635 or visit www.ReaderService.com.

*Terms and prices subject to change without notice. Prices do not include applicable taxes. Sales tax applicable in N.Y. Canadian residents will be charged applicable taxes. Offer not valid in Quebec. This offer is limited to one order per household. Books received may not be as shown. Not valid for current subscribers to Harlequin Desire books. All orders subject to approval. Credit or debit balances in a customer's account(s) may be offset by any other outstanding balance owed by or to the customer. Please allow 4 to 6 weeks for delivery. Offer available while quantities last.

Your Privacy—The Reader Service is committed to protecting your privacy. Our Privacy Policy is available online at www.ReaderService.com or upon request from the Reader Service.

We make a portion of our mailing list available to reputable third parties that offer products we believe may interest you. If you prefer that we not exchange your name with third parties, or if you wish to clarify or modify your communication preferences, please visit us at www.ReaderService.com/consumerchoice or write to us at Reader Service Preference Service, P.O. Box 9062, Buffalo, NY 14240-9062. Include your complete name and address.

HDI7R3

That damn buzz passed from him to her and ignited the flames low in her belly.

"When I get back to the office, you will officially become a client," Reame said in a husky voice. "But you're not my client...yet."

His words made no sense, but she did notice that he was looking at her like he wanted to kiss her.

Reame gripped her hips. She felt his heat and... Wow...

God and heaven.

Teeth scraped and lips soothed, tongues swirled and whirled, and heat, lazy heat, spread through her limbs and slid into her veins. Reame was kissing her, and time and space shifted.

It felt natural for her legs to wind around his waist, to lock her arms around his neck and take what she'd been fantasizing about. Kissing Reame was better than she'd imagined—she was finally experiencing all those fuzzy feels romance books described.

It felt perfect. It felt right.

Reame jerked his mouth off hers and their eyes connected, his intense, blazing with hot green fire.

She wanted him… She never wanted anybody. And never this much.

"Holy crap—"

Reame stiffened in her arms and Lachlyn looked over his shoulder to the now-open door to where her brother stood, half in and half out of the room. Lachlyn slid down Reame's hard body. She pushed her bangs off her forehead and released a deep breath, grateful that Reame shielded her from Linc.

Lachlyn touched her swollen lips and glanced down at her chest, where her hard nipples pushed against the fabric of her lacy bra and thin T-shirt. She couldn't possibly look more turned-on if she tried.

Lachlyn couldn't look at her brother, but he sounded thoroughly amused. "Want me to go away and come back in fifteen?"

Reame looked at her and, along with desire, she thought she saw regret in his eyes. He slowly shook his head. "No, we're done."

Lachlyn met his eyes and nodded her agreement.

Yes, they were done. They had to be.

Don't miss
ONE NIGHT TO FOREVER by Joss Wood,
*part of her **BALLANTYNE BILLIONAIRES** series!*

Available May 2018 wherever
Harlequin® Desire books and ebooks are sold.

www.Harlequin.com

Want to give in to temptation with
steamy tales of irresistible desire?

Check out **Harlequin® Presents®**,
Harlequin® Desire and
Harlequin® Kimani™ Romance books!

New books available every month!

CONNECT WITH US AT:

Harlequin.com/Community

 Facebook.com/HarlequinBooks

 Twitter.com/HarlequinBooks

 Instagram.com/HarlequinBooks

 Pinterest.com/HarlequinBooks

ReaderService.com

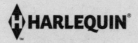

**ROMANCE WHEN
YOU NEED IT**

PGENRE2017